Ian Watson was born on Tyneside in 1943. He studied English at Balliol College, Oxford. His first speculative fiction stories were stimulated by his three-year stay as a lecturer in Japan. In 1969 *Roof Garden Under Saturn*, a short story, was published in *New Worlds* magazine, and since then his stories have appeared in various magazines and anthologies. They have been published in book form in three collections, *The Very Slow Time Machine*, *Sunstroke* and *Slow Birds*.

Ian Watson's first novel, *The Embedding*, was published in 1973 and received enormous critical acclaim. His second novel, *The Jonah Kit*, became a British Science Fiction Award winner as well as confirming his position in the front rank of contemporary British writers. He has been features editor of the journal *Foundation* since 1975 and a full-time writer since 1976.

By the same author

IAN WATSON

The Book of Being

GRAFTON BOOKS
A Division of the Collins Publishing Group

LONDON GLASGOW
TORONTO SYDNEY AUCKLAND

Grafton Books
A Division of the Collins Publishing Group
8 Grafton Street, London W1X 3LA

Published by Grafton Books 1986

First published in Great Britain by
Victor Gollancz Ltd 1985

ISBN 0-586-06389-7

Printed and bound in Great Britain by
Collins, Glasgow

Set in Plantin

Contents

PART ONE
Tam's Pots

So it was as a child just a quarter short of my third year that I was installed in the temple of the black current in downtown Pecawar. I'd be public proof of how we could all be saved by the grace of the Worm, courtesy of its *Ka*-store. Whilst in actual fact the whole human cosmos was about to come to a sticky end, maybe no longer than two years hence!

I soon called in the promise which Quaymistress Chanoose had rashly made; namely that in addition to my honour guard of guilds-women I might gather a few friends about me. I asked for Tam to come.

It may have been cruel to wrench Tam away from fair artistic Aladalia to dusty Pecawar. It might have been inconsiderate to ask him to squander his one-go on the river so that he could squire a mere child, in whom happened to have been reborn the young woman he had loved besottedly. Nevertheless I wanted him. I knew I would need the services of a loyal soul or two.

'Tam's a potter,' I told Chanoose. 'Doesn't Pecawar, baked by the sun, and the colour of clay already, need a potter to give it some bright glaze? Doesn't my temple need ornaments – such as vases for the flowers my pilgrims will bring? And splendid faience plates for them to pour coins into?'

I also requested the presence of Peli, the songful water-wife. Peli originally hailed from Aladalia too.

'It might be better,' replied Chanoose, 'if you chose your companions from different directions – not both from the same place! Can't you think of someone from Jangali or Tambimatu? That way you'd be forging symbolic ties. Two from Aladalia seems like favouritism.'

'I want Peli.' Her, I could trust. 'Besides, then Tam won't feel so lonely.' It almost sounded as if I was trying to fix up a marriage between Peli and Tam.

'Oh, as you please! I don't suppose it matters; if it'll make you happy.'

We were talking in the audience chamber – alias throne room – of my temple. Let me describe the edifice.

It had been a disused spice warehouse, which was swiftly but quite elegantly converted by masons, carpenters and furnishers hired by the guild. The rear backed directly on to the river; a new covered verandah overlooked the water. The front faced Pemba Avenue, which converges on Zanzyba Road close to the Café of the Seasons. The claybrick frontage was dolled up with outriding sandstone columns to provide a roofed arcade, where food hawkers and lemonade lads soon took up residence along with various licensed souvenir vendors; chief amongst whom was the bookstall proprietor who held the temple franchise to sell copies of *The Book of the River*. (This was shortly going to be reprinted with my private afterword included, according to Chanoose.)

A grand flight of steps bridged the arcade, running up to an entry porch above. These steps were clad with thin flags of purple Melonby marble to prevent the feet of countless pilgrims from wearing them away too soon. There hadn't been enough stock within easy reach of Pecawar to build the steps of solid marble. In any case, think of the expense. And the effect was the same.

In this manner the entrance was relocated one storey upward – so as to convey a sense of ascendance. Yet the steps mustn't be too steep; nor must they commence in the

10

middle of Pemba Avenue. Consequently the entry porch had to be recessed well behind the original wall. This meant that busy teams of craftsmen had their work cut out reconstructing a lot of the interior to accommodate stairway, upper-floor porch and foyer. They laboured overtime and even through the nights by lamplight at double rates.

My audience chamber, which led off the foyer, was mostly panelled with rich gildenwood. A couple of tapestries covered stretches of cheaper old wood. One of these tapestries was a rather abstract representation of desert dunes; it flowed nicely into the gildenwood. The other tapestry pictured a fishmask regatta at a fanciful Gangee. I was assured that weavers would soon set to work upon thoroughly relevant new tapestries depicting scenes from my past life – such as how I had ridden in the mouth of the Worm with the sun's rays shining forth from my ring. Or how I had confronted a giant croaker in the jungle, me armed only with a sharpened wand (the weavers would need me to be holding something, for the composition). Or even how I had been martyred (but surely not cowering under a bed?).

And in my audience chamber upon a dais, I had a tiny tot-size throne of rubyvein with a fat tasselled cushion for my bum.

The honour guard – who doubled as temple officials – occupied the remainder of that upper storey. My own private living quarters were down below; as were those of my parents, various empty rooms destined for my personal retinue, and the temple treasury – which, when I moved in, was also empty. Short of jumping into the river off the verandah I could only leave my new home by mounting and using the main entrance, which immediately involved an escort; this kept me conveniently in my place.

It had been decided not to include a kitchen in the

11

temple. A tad undignified, perhaps, to have smells of stew wafting over my waiting worshippers? Thus meals were ordered in from outside; and mine were generally cool by the time they reached me. This was a fatuous stratagem, since the whole place reeked of spices. All of the surviving fabric was imbued; and doubtless there was a carpet of spice dust a thumbnail deep beneath the ground floor. A thorough scrub-out with soap didn't make one whit of difference.

When eventually there was enough money in the coffers, the idea was to erect a really stately temple mostly of Melonby marble, with a large courtyard, somewhere out in the suburbs. Meanwhile I must make do with this converted warehouse, which looked sumptuous enough so long as you didn't try to prise off the veneer, and made believe that the powerful odour was some kind of incense as in old tales.

And why not make believe? In spite of new gildenwood panelling and those tapestries which blanketed the surviving old wood, for some reason the smell of spice seemed particularly noticeable in my throne room. This set me to wondering whether visitors from other towns might imagine that it emanated from my presence, diffusing hence to spread throughout the town! Just so had I once imagined that Dad, in his working clothes, was the source and origin of Pecawar's native aroma.

Which brings me to the matter of Dad himself. His was a slightly tragic case, which I was truly sorry to see – albeit that I was to blame. Me; and Chanoose's machinations in making me a priestess.

Mum was up; Dad down. Mum revelled in the glory. She was proud and committed. Dad, on the other hand, was out of a job – since he could hardly continue counting spice sacks and totting up ledgers now that his daughter was a high priestess. Worse, he was out of a job inside a former warehouse where every sniff reminded him of his previous independence. He who had ever held his job at arm's length, far from family matters – save for those excursions with Narya during the war – now had his nose rubbed in empty reminders of the past; with wife and 'false' daughter always close at hand. However, he put a brave face on necessity. Mum and Dad occupied a decent suite adjacent to my own; and whilst Mum found much to busy herself with in improving the accoutrements of the temple, Dad gravitated inevitably (though a little grimly) towards the counting house. Soon he was totting up donated fish-coins with wry perseverance and improving the book-keeping.

By now our family house had become a museum. Mum happily countenanced this and acted as advisor in the matter. Dad refused to go back there or have anything to do with this conversion of his former home into a tramping place for curious strangers.

So now we had two prongs of pilgrimage: the temple, and our house along the dusty lane. A third holy place could obviously be the cemetery where Yaleen's murdered body lay – Must keep pilgrims busy! Give them a full itinerary! – and about this, debate grew a little heated, with me entering the fray.

It was a lamplit evening in my throne room, and Chanoose had a pronouncement to make. Present to hear it were myself, Mum and Dad – and Donnah, captain of the guard and major-domo of the temple.

Donnah was a tall busty redhead, with noteworthy muscles and strapping shoulders, whose attitude to me – the holy brat – I still hadn't quite figured out. By her accent Donnah was from further north. Sarjoy or somewhere. She managed to be both extremely protective, to which end she always wore a four-shot Guineamoy pistol, and quite off-hand in her duties as major-domo; which was how Mum found an easy entrée into temple management. To be sure, the temple was Donnah's command; but it wasn't exactly a boat, to be kept spick and span. I suspected that Donnah was the restless sort and may have felt miffed to be made captain of a revamped warehouse – never mind that she was performing sterling service for her guild: its prestige, its revenues. In Donnah, I fancied, Chanoose had appointed someone who wouldn't become a kind of rival quaymistress in town. Yet Donnah's inner person remained opaque to me; far more so than dear conniving Chanoose. Of one thing I was certain: Donnah wouldn't allow me to manipulate her, or gain the upper hand.

I perched on my throne. The others squatted on quilted floor-cushions, Jay-Jay guildhall-style, except for Chanoose who stood.

'We must decide about the cemetery,' she declared. Donnah immediately nodded agreement. 'Yaleen's grave ought to be visited.'

'That could be difficult,' I pointed out, 'seeing as I'm sunk in sand in an unmarked spot.'

'We must mark it, then.'

'And how would you find it, to mark it?'

Mum spoke up. 'I'm sure *I* haven't forgotten the spot.' Chanoose smiled brightly at her.

'Maybe my death-box already broke surface and got burnt,' I said.

'Oh no.' Chanoose shook her head. 'Impossible. Far too soon. Now as to a memorial – '

'But the sands shift,' said Dad. 'The memorial would lean. It might fall over. That isn't very dignified.'

'In that case,' suggested Donnah, 'maybe we should

retrieve the body and build a proper marble tomb nearby? With the corpse embalmed within?'

Dad twisted his hands about. 'I doubt if the people of Pecawar would consider a tomb all that proper! You should leave her poor body be. She was my daughter – I do have a right to say this!'

'I still am your daughter, Dad.'

Dad looked bewildered for a moment. He sighed; subsided.

'It seems to me,' I went on, 'speaking as your priestess, that the whole idea's nonsense. It defeats the purpose of why I'm here in this temple. What we're concerned with is *Ka*s, not bodies. Not that I'm disparaging bodies! But damn it, I've had three of them by now.'

'You are the three-in-one,' said Chanoose, amiably toying with this new phrase. 'Three bodies! Surely you can spare one of them for cult purposes?'

'No, no, no. It's stupid.'

We argued a while; and to my surprise I won. The guild would not, after all, exhume my semi-mummified remains from the sands. Instead they would merely affix a plaque to the stone archway of the graveyard. Then of course eager pilgrims could always hope that a fierce gale might blow up on the night before their visit. The corpse of Yaleen might possibly surface in its death-box specially for them. The Rods could rake in some spare cash, if they were ingenious. They could try to sell relics. Splinters. Ashes. Hanks of hair.

Visits! By pilgrims! Now we come to the meat of my role as priestess (as opposed to the bones in the sand).

The idea was *not* that I should actually proclaim to visitors, even though I'd had a fair amount of practice at this while I was a cherub in Venezia. Visitors were expected to buy my book, to receive my message. They practically

15

had to flash a copy to gain admission. And by now Chanoose and I (and Dad) had sorted out the vexed question of royalties, not wholly to my satisfaction . . .

A word about this. The guild had invested heavily in me; so the cost must be amortized. One source of revenue was straight donations to the temple. Another was entrance fees to our house – cash which seemed to be swallowed up in the cost of caretaking! A third source was profit from my book, less the six per cent which I could keep as my private purse. This was a far cry from the fifty-fifty split which Chanoose had brashly offered at my graveside; but then circumstances had altered radically, hadn't they? As financial consultant to myself and the temple, Dad actually concurred in this arrangement, though he insisted on a fatter split in a few years' time. Meanwhile he and Mum were living free. As was I. And what could I possibly spend money on? If I did set my heart on something, said he, far better to soak the temple for expenses and keep my purse intact. (True, temple expenses would have to be met from the same sources – and I later discovered that such expenses included the cost of Tam's fare to Pecawar; the guild wasn't picking up the tab.)

Enough of fins and fish! As I say, the guild were wary of any proclamations I might make; but I must needs be present twice a day in my throne room for audiences, with Donnah and a couple of guards standing by.

Goodness, did some visitors try my patience – no matter how goodly a store of that commodity I'd garnered during the two years while I was pretending to be a normal infant! A stooped old lady would approach, clutching her copy of the book. She would cast a handful of fins into the offering bowl, then address me as if I was some fortune teller.

'My eldest daughter – Shinova, you know – she died of a fever in Port Barbra these nineteen years since. Did you

16

meet her in yon *Ka*-store? Is she well and happy? Will I join her when I die? And it won't be long now, not the way I felt in my heart this Winter . . . I shouldn't want to go to yon Eeden, and never see my flesh again. If Shinny's in your *Ka*-store, give me to drink, child wonder, tiny joy!'

'Have you ever drunk of the black current before, Mother?'

'Never.'

'Drink now.'

One of my attendants would present this old biddy with a slug of darkness in a little glass cup. Exit another satisfied customer, wiping her lips. Her name and address would be registered for temple records; she was enrolled.

Other petitioners were sharper-brained. Indeed I suppose the majority were, so I shouldn't be too anecdotal. But I had to pack a lot of people into these sessions, and she was the sort who stood out.

Soon a flood of local landlubber women were joining the new cult; and Chanoose reported delightedly that much the same was happening in other towns, where proxies of mine administered the dose. For some reason Guineamoy seemed a tough nut to crack – while north of Aladalia progress was hampered somewhat by an absence of the black stuff locally. Barrels of black current had to be boated to Port Firsthome and beyond.

'I do hope,' I remarked to Chanoose one day, 'that the black current can replenish itself quickly enough!'

'How do you mean?'

'At this rate we might drink it dry.'

'You can't be serious. We're only taking a tiny portion. And it's allowing us. No boat sailing out to the midstream for fresh supplies has met any bother. Besides – '

'Okay, just a joke.'

'This isn't a joking matter.'

'Sorry.'

'Our volunteers are working double-time at Aladalia to supply the northernmost towns.'

'Ah, the brave black current bucket brigade.' I wondered who was paying them. Me, probably.

'Yes, brave indeed! But we aren't rushing recklessly.'

'I didn't suppose you would be.'

'Still, we'll have to start enrolling men before too long; or we might lose impetus. That reminds me: this fellow of yours, Tam, is starting upstream soon. He's booked passage.'

'Glad to hear it. But *not* so glad that the one thing reminds you of the other! I recall you fancying how my father's might be a convenient toe to dip in the water, to see if he got stung. So it's to be Tam's toe now: is that your idea?'

'It'll have to be *some* man's toe, sooner or later. Will the current accept men? Thereby hangs our whole enterprise in the long run. Obviously the man in question should be somebody you're close to, so that the current can share your concern. Speaking of which: have there been any intimations lately, which you've neglected to mention? Any messages, contacts?'

'I've been a little busy of late, Chanoose. Or hadn't you noticed?'

'Not when you're asleep, you haven't. I don't think you're trying. It's a priestess's duty to mediate with . . . whatever she's priestess of.'

'So maybe the Worm's still mulling over all I told it.'

'You could enquire.'

'I'm bloody tired when I get to bed. I probably sleep too deeply. I'm only going on three years old, remember? And maybe our Worm has its work cut out with all these *Ka*s pouring in.'

18

'Rubbish. Women aren't dropping dead just because they drink the current.'

'Okay, okay. Yawn, yawn. So when's Tam due to sail? Not, I hasten to add, so that he can become the first male toe in the water!'

'In a week or so.'

It was Peli who arrived in Pecawar first; and what a reunion that was.

The last time we'd seen each other was when the nameless ketch, renamed *Yaleen*, sailed me out to the Worm's head up beyond Tambimatu. But naturally I wasn't the same Yaleen as Peli had bidden adieu to back then. My face was another's. And I had shrunk considerably! So when Peli bustled into my quarters late one afternoon, shown the way by Lana, one of the guards, my friend halted as if aghast at what she beheld – she was hamming it up a bit – then she burst out into joyful laughter.

'Oh I *knew*!' she whooped. 'But it's one thing knowing, and another thing seeing!' She snatched me up into the air and spun round, hugging me; which almost made Lana have a fit.

'Hey, *hey*!' I protested. 'I'm fragile. I break easy.'

'What: *you*?'

'Okay, so I'm not particularly.'

'Only when you had a hangover!'

'But I have me, um, dignity to think about.' And I winked full in her big red burly face, loving the sight of it.

'You may depart,' I told Lana; who did.

'Quite the princess!' Peli declared.

'You mean priestess. You don't mind, do you, Peli?'

'What, mind you being a priestess?'

'No, you noddle. Mind being dragged all the way here. Being hauled off the river. I need friends, Peli.'

19

She had sobered. 'I guessed as much. What for?' she whispered.

'I'm hemmed in. I'm smothered with attention. Watched. Just yet I don't know what's best to do – '

'But when you do, I'll be here to help.' Peli looked round my quarters, noting the child-size bed, the profusion of flockity rugs to cushion any falls, the doors to the river verandah with their great bolts set out of reach, my bookcase crammed with Ajelobo romances, my antique ivorybone scritoire with a pile of blank paper and a pot of ink in it . . .

'Wondering where I keep my toys?'

She grinned. 'Wondering where you keep the booze.'

'Aha.' I headed for the brass bell mounted over my bed and clanged it. Lana reappeared speedily. 'What'll it be, then?' I asked Peli.

'A drop of ginger spirit wouldn't come amiss.'

'A bottle of,' I told Lana. 'Plus a spiced ale for myself.'

'A small one?'

'But of course.'

Lana nodded, and soon returned with the drinks on a copper tray. Peli and I settled to talk the rest of the afternoon away; and the evening too till dinner time.

Peli had of course noted the pile of paper waiting to be inked. 'Another book?' she enquired eventually. I thought it had taken her rather a long while to ask. 'Mmm. This time I think it would be wise to make *two* copies.'

'Why's that?'

'One to smuggle out. Somehow or other.'

'Oh, the guard frisked me on the way in – looking for hidden hatchets or bludgeons, I thought. Do you mean it's the same when you leave? Hey, I do *get out*, don't I? I mean, I'm allowed into town?'

'You're allowed. No problem. But they'll be leery of what you might take out *with* you. Nobody could slip a whole wad of paper past the guard, and page by page'll take ages. Still, a page at a time is how the copy'll have to be made if prying eyes aren't to see.'

'Sounds difficult.' Peli glanced at the verandah door.

'They keep an eye on the water. No rowboat could sneak up.'

'Sounds downright impossible.'

'Oh, come off it. Is this Peli talking? There's bound to be a way. But the first stage is to get the copy made – whilst I'm busy writing the damn book.'

She looked unaccountably troubled. 'Is this new book of yours really so important?'

'Oh, merely to untold millions of people on lots of other worlds, whose brains the Godmind means to fry. Just *that* important.'

'Hmm. Important enough.'

'Right now we're only intent on saving ourselves. No one but me has any concept of other worlds.'

'Yes I know that, but do you honestly think a book could alter anything? That's what I wonder.' Peli poured herself more ginger spirit, a bit urgently. Myself, I'd long since quaffed my spiced ale. Any more booze at the moment would send a little girl to sleep; though with dinner to soak it up I might manage another small ale later. 'I mean, for starters there's the whole problem of how to get our own *men* into the *Ka*-store! Not to mention that mob on the west bank. Aren't you being too ambitious? I honestly don't see what any of us could *do* for a hundred other worlds.' (That was two 'honestly's in the span of a minute. So what was Peli being *dis*honest about?)

'Neither do I! Not yet. But you surely aren't saying you don't even *want* to try to help save hundreds of millions of people? I don't know how – but *somehow*! For a start, by making everyone aware.'

Peli looked downright miserable. 'Yaleen, what I'm saying . . . as regards copying your book . . . is that I just don't write too well. Or read, for that matter. In fact, I just *don't*. Read and write. Can't,' she mumbled.

'Oh grief.' I didn't know what to say. I hadn't for one moment suspected. And I don't suppose that anybody else ever had; for I could see how much this confession cost her. 'Oh Peli, I'm sorry.'

'I go cross-eyed when I see words written down. The letters jump around and do dances.' She wouldn't meet my eyes.

'And you from Aladalia, Peli.'

'Where everyone is so brilliant! Don't I know it? That's why I became a riverwoman. But at least, if I can't read, I can sing.'

I had to smother a chuckle. 'Of course you can.'

'But I'm still ruddy useless to you. It was a waste of time asking me here.'

'No! Don't say so! I haven't been able to confide in anyone till now. I need you, Peli.'

'Can't copy your book, though.'

No, and I couldn't copy it either. I already had enough other duties on my plate. Once I actually started writing, my spare time would be gobbled up.

'We'll think of something. You and I,' I assured her. 'Don't fret; I really do need you here.'

Didn't I just! It seemed to me a fair bet that the guild wouldn't publish this next book uncensored. They might be selective, or they might simply sit on the book. I could be wrong, but I wasn't going to risk it. So: how to smuggle a copy out, supposing one could be made?

How could it reach a printing press? And how could

22

copies get distributed – with the guild in charge of all cargoes? Peli was going to have to be a smuggler, and a courier, and more. Ah yes: I would pretend to quarrel with Peli. I would send her away with a flea in her ear, and my book in her duffle bag. Somehow.

Peli brightened. She drained her glass and refilled it with the last from the bottle. 'Let's sing a song for old times' sake, eh?'

'Why not?' said I. So we carolled our way through till it was time for dinner, which luckily for the ears of anyone musical in the neighbourhood wasn't too long a-coming.

Dinner was served in Mum's and Dad's suite, and consisted of pig's kidney and tomato kebabs on a bed of saffron rice; all of which no doubt had been hot enough when it set out from the café. Peli switched to ale, and I got my hands on a second small mug too.

I could see that Dad took to Peli, though the booze made her distinctly brash and chortly – I guess she was rebuilding her self-esteem after the confession of illiteracy. Oh what, I wondered, would Dad – who could read a whole page of spidery writing and crabbed numbers in two flicks of a lamb's tail – have thought of *that*? Oddly enough, I didn't think he would have minded. Mum, on the other hand, merely tolerated Peli. Mum put up with her.

It was only during dessert (of sorbet blancmange) that I realized that Peli couldn't possibly have read *The Book of the River*. She surely wouldn't have asked any riversister to read it aloud to her! This meant there must be great gaps in her knowledge of my adventures, ones which she hadn't enquired into while we were chewing the fat earlier on; so as not to betray herself. *I'd* mainly been bringing her up to date on what had happened since Edrick murdered me.

I determined to puzzle out what these gaps must be and

try to plug them as diplomatically as possible during the course of the next few weeks.

The very next day, in between my stints in the throne room, I began to write *The Book of the Stars*.

It wasn't easy at first. I admit to a few false starts. For here was I, writing about how Tam suddenly hove into sight in Aladalia whilst I was busy writing *The Book of the River*; and lo, Tam was about to sail into view once again, this time ex Aladalia and at my own behest! So events seemed curiously overlaid, as if I were suffering from double vision. Also, I was writing about happenings which seemed fairly remote to me, who had spent two 'extra' years in between on Earth and its Moon; but to Tam and Peli and everyone else these same happenings were much more recent. I'd looped back through time; they hadn't.

Soon I was quite intoxicated with my reconstruction of the past. It came as something of a shock when Chanoose announced one day, 'Your Tam's due tomorrow noon, aboard the *Merry Mandolin*.'

Peli, I hasten to add, had been allowed to turn up at the temple without prior advertisement. So no doubt Chanoose said this to get in my good books. Literally! Plain to see that I'd begun writing something. Chanoose and Donnah were well aware that I intended to; so if I had tried to conceal what I was up to, I'm sure this would have roused suspicions. (The copy was what I intended to conceal; howsoever it got done.) Consequently I tackled the job in a spirit of brazen privacy. The privacy component was that I kept my finished copy locked up safely in my scritoire, and made no bones about not letting people kibitz on my work in progress. The brazen part was that I tore up numerous sheets of spoiled paper, cursing roundly in my kiddy voice. This display of artistic temperament deterred enquiries,

24

but more importantly I noted how all such torn scraps disappeared from the straw trash bucket with an efficiency which I ascribed not so much to impassioned tidiness on the part of Lana and company, as to a desire to oversee all of my abortive scribblings. Once I got into my stride – and was in fact writing smoothly – I catered to this appetite by scrawling a few extra irrelevant lines especially to tear up.

The basket squatted beside my scritoire like a big hairy ear hoping to eavesdrop; but I wasn't worried that eyes would pry into the scritoire itself whilst I was otherwise engaged being priestess. Peli mightn't be able to write but she could certainly perform other neat marvels with her fingers. In town she had purchased a complicated lock, cunningly crafted in Guineamoy. This, she substituted skilfully for the lock in the scritoire lid as supplied, to which I assumed Donnah would have kept a spare key. I always wore the new key round my neck.

If Chanoose was hoping to ingratiate herself, that was her mistake. Forewarned, I insisted on going to meet Tam when he docked the next day. And why not, indeed? I was sick of sitting on my backside in the temple. Sitting at my scritoire. (I'd found that I genuinely *had* to turf Peli out while I was composing my narrative, by the way, so maybe my temperaments weren't all pretence.) Sitting on my throne. Sitting at the dinner table. And occasionally sitting out on the verandah, either playing cards with Peli and Dad, or else with my nose in a romance; before tossing it aside – the romance, that is! – to get on writing my own romance. I had to get out!

Halfway through the next morning's audience, I rose and quit; went down to my quarters to pace the verandah.

Presently a brig schooner drifted into view, angling in towards the shore. At that distance I couldn't quite read the words painted on the side, but a flag hung over the stern from the ensign staff with a design stitched on it which was either a semitone sign or else the outline of a mandolin. I ran indoors and clanged my bell.

Donnah had decreed that I should be escorted through the streets to the docks with all due dignity; namely, perched shoulder-high in a padded chair strapped to poles. So much did my litter rock and bob and undulate upon that journey that for a while I, who had never been water-sick but once – aboard the *Sally Argent*, and then not because of waves – feared that I might turn up at the quayside green and puking. However, I gritted my teeth and even managed to grin and wave my free hand to passers-by who stopped to applaud and blow kisses and fall in behind us; with my other hand I had to clutch the chair-arm.

Still, at least by this method we proceeded apace. Once we were within sight of the quay, with the *Merry Mandolin* yet to heave its mooring ropes ashore, I cried, 'Set me down! I'll walk from here!' And so I did, with my guards cordoning me from the wake of townsfolk.

When Tam appeared at the head of the gangplank – a huge bag in each hand – he just stood there for upward of a minute blocking the way. I was waiting at the bottom, with Donnah and her gang. Behind, a fair throng of spectators loomed. Yet Tam didn't seem to notice any of us. He was only seeing – well, he told me this subsequently when we were walking back to the temple together; with his bags riding in my chair rather than me, to Donnah's chagrin – he was only seeing that gangplank which led from water on to land. He was seeing the fact that whilst he stayed aboard the *Merry Mandolin*, he could still sail anywhere – even all the way back home to Aladalia. But once he crossed that bridge, he would be marooned ashore. Tam was sure he had left something in his cabin; and indeed he had. It wasn't anything tangible, though. What he had left was the way back home. That was why he hesitated for so long.

He descended. We shook hands – quaintly, his big lumpy hand making mine disappear. I argued with Donnah a bit. The guards hoisted his bags; we set off.

I soon heard his confession. 'But it's so wonderful to be here with you!' he insisted. He was stooping over me from what now seemed to me a hugely gangly height. 'That you should have asked for me out of everyone – well, well!' His voice sank softly so that only I should hear. 'I have the fleuradieu you sent me, pressed and dried in my luggage – and I have a surprise as well. A present. I never thought I'd actually deliver it. I hoped you might come across its like in some far town one day, and realize that it was for you.'

'That sounds delightfully mysterious.'

'The mystery is *you*, Yaleen.'

He seemed genuinely happy when he said these things. I decided that this was because he had at last found a way of fulfilling his impossible love for me. He could be near me, adoring me to his heart's content and even touching me, as a big brother a sister; our relationship had suddenly been blessed with innocence. Now he was exempt from any ordinary expectations a lover might have had of him, where he might have fallen short. Equally, no one else could ever win me from him, since I was physically unwinnable. No need for jealousy. He was cured, redeemed, his aching ecstatic heart's wound salved.

Or so I told myself while he escorted me, nudging my guards into the background merely by the way he walked. At first I had felt qualms about that business at the gangplank, as he explained it; yet now I congratulated myself somewhat.

Till Tam sniffed the air anxiously. 'It's so dry here,' he said, more to himself than to me.

'Yes? Pecawar's near the desert.'

Tam's feet scuffed the dust. His eyes assessed a warehouse built of sandstone blocks which we were passing.

'Dry. Even the river was dusty.'

'What's wrong, Tam? It's a different place, that's all. Aladalia isn't the whole world. If you'd wedded, you'd have had to – '

'I wedded my art.'

'Which you can practise here as easily as . . .' I faltered. For in that moment I had seen what he was seeing.

'Clay,' he murmured. 'A potter needs clay. And not just any sort of mud, either! I need kaolin clay and petuntse clay. Kaolin is decomposed granite, and petuntse is decayed feldspar which melts into glass. That's if I want to craft real porcelain . . . For soft pasteware I'd only need chalk, white clay and frit. But frit's made up of gypsum, salt, soda and quartz sand. Anyhow, pasteware scratches easy and picks up grease marks . . . And if I just wanted to craft faience or majolica, I'd still need the right sort of soft earth, wouldn't I? It's so arid here. All dust and sand. I hadn't realized.'

'Whatever you need, the guild will get.'

Tam laughed. 'What, tubs of the right kinds of clay all the way from Aladalia?'

'Why not?'

'They'd probably dry out. Anyway, it isn't the sort of stuff you buy in any old quayside shop. It has to be sought. A potter should know his clay like his own flesh, or else he botches. He turns out second-best that cracks and crazes.'

'Can't you write to friends in Aladalia, saying exactly what you need?'

'And wait weeks and weeks, and meantime change my

28

plans? No, a potter should work with the local clay that he's in touch with.' His shoe grooved the surface of the street. 'Dust and sand all around me. Oh well, I guess I can try my hand at brickwork. Why not? I'll be a big fish in a pond that's otherwise empty.' He grinned lamely.

But of course I didn't yet know the half of it; and it was Peli who got Tam to explain fully over dinner, which we three ate privately that evening in my own chamber.

Just before the meal was served, he presented me with his gift: a bundle of straw tied with twine. Within was a mass of chicken feathers. And nestling inside those . . . a fragile translucent white bowl.

A bowl about the size of Tam's hand. The sort of bowl that ought only to hold clear water with a single green leaf afloat. Or only air. There was already something floating at the bottom of the bowl beneath the glaze: a dark violet fleuradieu, last flower of deepening winter. For a moment I thought this was the very bloom which I had sent to Tam by way of goodbye. But no; it was painted exquisitely on the porcelain.

'Why, Tam! It's beautiful. No, it's *more* than beautiful. Did you really craft this?'

'Who else? It's part of a series showing all the hues of the farewell flower from summer's powder-blue to the midnight blue of year's end.'

'How did you manage it?'

He shuffled his big feet and twisted his knobbly hands about. Lana had finished setting out some lacquer food boxes for us. She said, 'Better fetch a brush and pan for the feathers, hadn't I?'

'No. Just leave us, will you?'

When she'd gone, Tam said, 'How indeed? Well, when you sent that flower, Yaleen, something altered in me.

29

This emblem . . . purified my art; enhanced it. It's only a little while since; it's a big change, I'd say.'

'A breakthrough?' queried Peli.

'*Hardly* the word a potter would use!' Tam chuckled and pinged the bowl with his fingernail.

'Don't!' cried Peli in alarm.

'It won't shatter unless you chuck it across the room. It's frail but strong, as an eggshell is. A fat hen could sit on it. Talking of chickens and eggs, let's eat. I'm starving.'

We took the lids off the food boxes only to find that we'd been served with raw fish, Spanglestream-style. Obviously this was a new experience for Tam. The fish of the northern reaches are coarse and indelicate compared with those of the south. Northerly fish need frying, boiling or barbecueing. True, we didn't have such delicacies as hoke or pollfish or ajil in Pecawar waters, either. But a few species made passable substitutes. What's more, the new Spanglestream-style restaurant whose fare we were sampling that evening had begun to experiment with importing the yellow pollfish and madder hoke alive in nets towed behind boats – though frankly these fish didn't seem to travel too happily; their flesh became a tad lacklustre en route.

Needless to say, I hadn't asked Donnah to order in a raw fish banquet for us; and I feared this was a bitter jest aimed at discomfiting the newly-arrived Tam who had never eaten such a thing in his life before. Maybe Chanoose had suggested our evening's menu to Donnah! Though raw fish was to my own taste – with reservations – I felt bound to apologize for the strange cuisine and assure Tam that it had nothing to do with regular Pecawar cuisine. I knew that he preferred spiced sausages, lamb pasties, faggots, blood pudding and such. If I'd had any sense, I should have foreseen something of the sort. I resolved to have a firm word with Donnah the next day.

But Tam claimed to enjoy all this raw fish, dipped in pepper and mustard sauces, as a novelty; and Peli pressed questions on her compatriot to make him feel very much the honoured guest; and perhaps distract him from what he was munching.

As she quizzed Tam, so the true – shall I say *enormity*? – of what I'd done in summoning him to Pecawar became more apparent.

Soon curious words and phrases were flying about, such as 'saggars' (which are fire-clay boxes) and 'biscuits' (which are what you call fired pots before they get glazed), and 'overglazing in a muffle fire' and 'burners who watch the kiln'.

'Burners?' I interrupted.

'People have to watch a fire to keep it constant.'

'How long do they do that for?'

'Sixty hours or thereabouts.'

'Oh. And your clay has to be crushed and churned first of all under a millstone?'

'Right; that's to render it soft and fine enough. Oh, I could fix up a grinding wheel sufficient to my needs, though I doubt I'll need one.'

'Why not?'

'No suitable clay. I'll have to turn my hand to brickware – or lustre and majolica. I reckon I can design a small kiln which won't need constant attention.'

'I'll pitch in,' said Peli. 'It'll give me something to do with my paws. Who knows, you setting up shop here could be quite like, well, the new Spanglestream restaurant opening!'

Tam surveyed a few slivers of fish remaining on his plate. 'Perhaps,' he sighed.

31

'Tam,' I said, 'I'll find you the clay you need – the clay to make fleuradieu porcelain! I promise I will.'

'But . . . how?'

'Tell me exactly what these kaolin and petuntse clays look like and smell like, and anything else about them.'

So he told me, though it isn't too easy to detail the hue and the feel of types of clay. I don't suppose he believed my promise, and I didn't explain further in case nothing did come of my plan.

That night I dreamed up a river for myself. That night I dreamed up a Worm. And the Worm rose from the depths of the waters; from the depths within me.

Hullo, Worm. Solved any riddles lately?

Hullo yourself. It isn't easy. Why is there a universe? Why is there a me? There's nothing to compare me with. Now if only I could contact another of my ilk . . .

Just what are you getting at?

'Tis but an idle notion.

Well, we don't have time for idle notions. What are we going to do about the Godmind, eh?

Aren't people doing it already, by booking tickets for my Ka-store? Pity there's an upper limit to the number of Kas I can swallow.

Say that again!

There's still room for you, if you get bored with being my priestess. Just jump in the river and I'll see to the rest.

You're having me on, Worm. You're trying to panic me. Admit it!

You can hardly expect me to swallow an infinite number of persons. Obviously there's an upper limit.

And it's large enough for everyone, I'll bet!

I do wish you would join me.

Sorry. Other duties call. And here's one of those duties, right off: I need clay.

Clay?

I need certain types of clay. Otherwise I'll have done the dirty on my friend Tam.

Explain.

So I did. *Will you search the memories in your Ka-store? Someone may know where to find kaolin and petuntse locally.*

No problem. I already know.

You do?

It's underwater, on the bed of my river. The stuff you call kaolin is about a league south of here. You'll find petuntse half a league beyond.

On the river bed? Sequestered by water and stingers, and by madness for any man . . .

The stuff's just offshore. A person could wade out and dig, if they held their breath.

Worm, it's time to talk about men.

Need some advice?

Don't be daft. I want you to promise that if Tam drinks of you you'll let him enter the river.

And my Ka-store too? I don't much care for the taste of the several dead Sons I swallowed.

Tam's different. He's gentle. Most of our men are, over here in the east. They've learned to flow with the world.

Hmm, I seem to recall they weren't so gentle recently — during a certain war.

And whose fault is that? You provoked the war!

Oh. So I did. And now you're asking for all men to drink of me and enter the Ka-store? That's what this request of yours implies.

Anything to get Tam his clay! Okay, so that's what I'm asking.

Hmm, but that would put an end to the female monopoly of

the river. Which would turn your own world upside-down and my Ka-store too. My whole inner landscape would alter. I don't think I like that.

If all our men get burnt up by the Godmind, and there are no more fathers, your inner landscape isn't going to get much more input from anyone!

My dear, I already contain multitudes of experience; so many are the Kas that I have swallowed.

Look: the Godmind wants to zap you. It'll find that a damn sight easier if it has access to crowds of dead men's Kas hereabouts.

True . . . I must survive. Therefore you must all survive in me, man and woman alike. You're right. Together we stand; together we'll unriddle the universe too, who knows?

Couldn't you accept men into the Ka-store but somehow forbid them access to the river? Except as now, for the one-go?

In that case how could Tam go plodging in the water to dig clay?

Oh. Um.

It's more of a problem than that, Yaleen . . . though I believe I spy a solution. Let me explain how it is at present that men are able to sail once and once only; and why twice brings madness and death. Down Tambimatu way, deep in the jungle, there's a little plant which catches insects to eat. This plant resembles toothy green jaws, yawning wide. If you touch the jaws once, nothing happens. A falling leaf might touch them once, or a drop of water. But if you touch them twice in the same manner, the jaws snap shut and devour. You see, something which touches twice is alive and active. I'm like that plant. I have arranged myself so as to ignore the first touch of a man – his first journey on my river.

And if the same fellow touches you twice, you seize him?

Just so. I could re-arrange myself so that a man's first brush with me kills him. That way men could drink of me, and gain

34

the Ka-store, but they couldn't ever stray off shore. Alternatively I could re-arrange myself so that men always have free access to the river.

Wait a minute! Are you saying that you could have fixed things during the war to give our whole army safe passage downstream? You could have kept your jaws shut?

Dear me. Those Sons might have sent reinforcements over.

Fat chance, with you back in position blocking the way across! You just wanted to spin things out.

Might I remind you, Yaleen, that you never asked any such favour of me?

True. Too damn true. Right then I could have curled up inside with embarrassment and grief. All that extra needless suffering; now I knew it for a fact. I wished I hadn't mentioned the matter.

Smug bug, I snarled.

Tem-per! You do want some clay for your boyfriend, don't you?

Yes. Sorry.

To resume: what I propose is that I shall turn out my lamp of death, which burns the moths of men. I shall extinguish it for a while. Your Tam will gain access to his clay. During this time you should build dikes in the shallows where the clay is, to hold the water back. You could drive in stakes to fix a wicker fence to, then pile bags of sand and heaps of stone along this fence. After that, bail out all the river-water. That part of the river bed will become land. Once that's done, thereafter I'll kill any man who ventures on the water at all. But all men shall drink of me and enter me at death – of the wisdom of that, I'm thoroughly persuaded. And only women shall sail.

Hang on. If men can't sail at all, how will they get wedded? How can they follow their fiancées to distant towns – hundreds of leagues in some cases? Lovers would have to aim their arrows much closer to home. What fun would a girl's wanderweeks be?

35

How could our towns be meshed by marriage, and the gene-pool stirred?

Just last week I gathered in the Ka of a woman who fell from the sky at Guineamoy.

What?

And from her I gather that some people have started experimenting with transport by steerable balloon. Excellent! Such balloons can carry lovers on honeymoon flights – how enchanting! A once in a lifetime experience. I think that solves the problem.

Balloons! There'd been some talk of military balloons, but I thought nothing had come of it . . .

Well I never did, I said.

Somebody else did. But she fell out – from a few hundred spans high. It's a really neat death. Elegant and graceful; bar the final splat. At the time she rather spoiled the effect by being so scared but in retrospect she can appreciate it better. If you want to die and join me and don't fancy drowning yourself, I'd seriously recommend leaping from a balloon. I assure you the last instant, when you get broken, is hardly noticeable.

Thanks for the tip. I was planning on surviving a while longer. In fact, I was planning on everybody, everywhere, surviving.

Thus totally trouncing the Godmind?

That's the general idea.

I need a fresh perspective on that, Yaleen. I've been trying to feel my way along the psylink to Earth, then out again in another direction. I need to find another Worm like me. Strength in numbers! Two eyes see deeper than one! Frankly I'm not having much luck on my own, so if you'd care to jump out of a balloon . . .

So that was it. The Worm wanted to project me through *Ka*-space once again.

Since I didn't answer, the Worm continued. *Meanwhile,*

36

that's the offer. Your men gain access to my Ka-store – *and lose the river entirely.*

All for a few barrels of clay . . .

No, not just for that. For the sake of every man alive. Actually, the Worm's offer ought to delight the river guild. They would continue to control the waterway.

Does my priestess so pledge, for her people?

Okay, agreed.

So be it. Now you carry on dreaming, and I'll show you the precise sites of those clay deposits.

At first Chanoose was incensed.

'You want to make mud pies? What is this, a complete reversion to childhood?'

'I intend to help my friend and companion get the materials he needs for his art. I *insist*. You yourself said we could do with some decent plates and vases in the temple.'

'I did?'

'Didn't you?' I asked innocently.

'So now you want a gang of riverwomen to dam and drain two stretches of river!'

'Ah, there's more to this, Quaymistress. And if I don't get my way, you won't get yours. What I've arranged with the Worm is as follows . . .' And I explained.

When I'd done, Chanoose said quietly, 'You impulsive imbecile. You really are incredible.' She spoke for form's sake only; I could see that her brain was pumping away nineteen to the dozen.

All of a sudden her eyes shone and she almost did a dance, there before my throne. 'Got it! Oh yes, I've got it! We time the work on these wretched dikes just long enough to *sail* all the captured Sons up north and ferry them over. That way, we shan't need half a 'jack army to escort them. We can keep the Sons chained up. We can take on local militia guards at each town. And while *that's* going on, we'll sail the whole 'jack army back home to Jangali – before they get too accustomed to foreign parts, or too restive.

'All those repatriated captives ought to mess up the west bank nicely. I shouldn't be surprised if half of them turn bandit, or try to overthrow their government. Then when everyone's well and truly back where they belong, hey presto, the dikes get finished. Your Worm opens its jaws again. Immediate embargo on the river! Brilliant, brilliant.' You'd think she had thought of it herself.

'Yes indeed! And we'll start putting men on the temple rolls. They'll accept the new set-up. We'll say it was the only way we could negotiate them a safe conduct into the *Ka*-store. By the way, the Worm's spot-on about balloon experiments. I think I'll slip news of those to the *Pecawar Publicizer* – '

'Including how you can fall out of them?'

'We'll have to tighten our grip on balloons. Invest in them; that's best. Hmm, which leaves us with one little problem: the black current only stretching just north of Aladalia . . . Never mind, never mind! You can have your dikes, Yaleen; rest easy. And *I* have signals to send.'

Departure of one satisfied customer. Or so I thought; she was back within a minute.

'Entirely forgot! This all drove it right out of my head. Double benefit, though, Yaleen! Recently a savant in Ajelobo approached the Guild. He's done a couple of services for us before. Sees things our way, he does. Well, he's been trying to analyse the nature of the current and the Godmind, based on what's been published already. So, what with the river being open to everyone for a while, we can sail him down here – '

'I'm not having anyone kibitzing over my shoulder!'

'Of course not, dear girl. He won't bother you. But if he's on hand when you finish *The Book of the Stars* – which I shan't even enquire about, so as not to irk you – how utterly convenient! Meantime, you could possibly bring yourself to iron out a few earlier points which puzzle him.'

'Such as how he's going to travel home afterwards? It's nigh on four hundred leagues to Ajelobo.'

'Not *quite*.'

'He won't be able to sail home.'

'Nor could the army, till now – and look how that problem's been solved. This fellow will probably return by balloon. Mind *you* – ' and Chanoose smartly changed the subject – 'if the Sons mount another invasion while the river's open, we could be in a mess – supposing the current let them plough through it on rafts. Which I doubt! Rafts haven't the draught of a boat, and the current's substance isn't ordinary. But even so! We'd better send all prisoners north securely battened under hatches in their chains, so that no westerners spy what's going on. We'll ferry them across at the last possible moment.'

'If the Sons wanted to invade, they could do it now – up north of Aladalia.'

'And doesn't every last jill and 'jack from Firsthome to Umdala know that, Yaleen, thanks to you! But really, that's way beyond the other enemy capital at Manhome North; so presumably the logistics forbid. That *was* your reasoning in leaving the far north unprotected, I take it?' (To which I said nothing.) Chanoose rubbed her hands. 'Fine, that's settled then.'

Off she went again. Five minutes later she was back, whistling *Masts High! Breezes Fly!*

'While the river's open to everyone, we'll hold a Grand Regatta here, that's what. We'll bring the date forward from the autumn. We'll invite men from Verrino and

39

Gangee. There'll be a grand initiation ceremony, with flags and bunting and masquerades and dances aboard the boats. It'll be a sort of official opening of the *Ka*-store to men – though obviously Pecawar men can join in earlier, and the 'jack army will be passing through beforehand.'

'Hang on! Aren't all our boats going to be full up with prisoners and armies?'

'I'm sure we can spare a few more vessels – if we suspend ordinary trade for a while, and cram those prisoners in tight.'

'Poor sods.'

'You don't mean that.'

'Maybe not.'

'That's how we'll do it.'

'Yes, but we're sending the Sons north under hatches for security reasons. Now we're going to have men dancing on deck – not to mention a whole 'jack army on the water.'

'Ah, but the command in the west will assume we've made a compact with the current. They won't know what sort, so long as they don't see their own men benefiting. *Actually*, it would be really neat if we could fool them into launching rafts across the current. Maybe we ought to feed some half-truths to the captives? Stuff they could blab when they got back home?'

'Some people can be too clever for their own good, Chanoose.'

'I thought that was *your* speciality, Yaleen.' Oh, she was indefatigable.

'So,' I said, 'we'll recruit lots of fellows from nearby towns by offering free trips to the Pecawar regatta.'

Chanoose looked amazed. 'Free? Who said anything about *free*? Does it cost nothing to build your dikes? Or to lay on a regatta? Plus a balloon – we'd better get hold of a balloon to accustom young lovers to the idea. Free indeed! What an impractical child you are.'

'Not quite! Maybe we ought to discuss the royalties for my next book here and now!' Here I was feeding *her* a half-truth; for I was pinning my hopes on the copy, not on the original.

She ignored this feint. 'I'm grateful for your comments. You point up the need for tight logistics.' And off she went, humming her tune.

After this I put on a spurt in my writing, other duties notwithstanding.

Time flowed.

I made one trip out of town, suitably escorted and on a day set by Chanoose, to point out to Tam and herself exactly where his clays were supposed to lie bedded underwater.

Naturally, the night before setting out, I had reminded the Worm of its promise to shut its man-trap down. Even so, my heart was in my throat when Tam waded out into the water, wearing anti-stinger gear, carrying a scoop-trowel and with a safety line around his waist. Breathing deep and ducking under, he brought up samples from the bottom, carried them ashore, dissected them with his gloves off, kneaded them, sniffed them, and even tasted them with the tip of his tongue before pronouncing them pukka. Probably; he wouldn't be absolutely sure till he had ground and fired the clay.

That evening Chanoose sent the signal for the 'jack army to set sail from Verrino; and for the prisoners to be freighted north, in the opposite direction. The 'jacks' voyage would span twice as many leagues as the captives covered, so the captives would be carried more slowly. Nobody wanted to erect temporary prison pens in the pastures by Aladalia.

41

Work commenced on the two dikes, and proceeded at a leisurely pace as ordained by Chanoose. Tam wasn't idle meanwhile; nor had he been so before that day when we sought out the clay. Already, with Peli's assistance, he had rigged up a grinding wheel and a potter's kick-wheel and had built a kiln to his own design.

The kiln was housed in a hut in a small yard abutting the north end of the temple, the only access to which was through the temple itself. A high claybrick wall tipped with jagged glass surrounded the yard, so I wouldn't be able to smuggle anything out by that route. Since the said area wasn't enormous, Tam stored finished wares in his own room, and a good number of items spilled into my own quarters. He wasn't producing porcelain (yet), but I liked his handiwork to be around.

To fuel the kiln he relied on quite costly nuts of coal imported by the sack from Guineamoy. Not for him the oil of Gangee which most people in Pecawar used for cooking and lighting and occasionally to take the chill off midwinter days. Occasionally; by no means everyone went in for such luxury. A Pecawar winter was never especially bitter. We preferred to shiver a bit (as I had shivered during the first week or so in the temple) and don a few more clothes. Wood, of course, was scanty in the region; imported timber was reserved for building and furnishing, not for fires.

So while I was turning out pages to lock in my trusty scritoire, Tam was creating nicely glazed brickware – painted with fleuradieus, to keep his hand in, he said. Soon he was selling his wares through one of the stalls along the arcade. And Peli, sweating at the kiln, seemed happy as a flutterbye which has found a saucer of syrup.

Obviously I couldn't ask Tam to take time off to copy my pages. He wrote a neat hand, but that wasn't what his hands were for. I certainly wouldn't impose on him for something slavishly routine.

The problem of how to get a copy made resolved itself in an unexpected way with the arrival of the savant from Ajelobo. Aye, resolved itself, and led to an awful outcome . . .

But I anticipate.

Already a fleet had conveyed our victorious army homeward, southward, through Pecawar. During the few days of the stop-over the scene was quite like the promised regatta, what with all those boats tied up at quays or anchored offshore, and the streets thronged with 'jacks in much gayer mood than when I'd spent time with them in Verrino.

My temple was also thronged; and many were the slugs of black current dispensed to ex-soldiers.

True, a certain stink of crowded travel hung about the 'jacks. (The guild was economizing on boats as much as possible, to meet all its commitments.) At least they weren't footsore, with holes in their boots and blisters and bunions. Their gait was sprightly. You'll recall my nagging sense of guilt in the matter. At least now I'd put things right – albeit I'd principally been thinking of how to supply Tam with petuntse and kaolin.

Thou shalt not congratulate thyself. Reality reared its head when I discovered that the hale and hearty 'jacks who strode jauntily along Pemba Avenue and crowded into my throne room were not the whole complement. A number of disabled 'jacks hadn't disembarked. Those sad fellows were lying in bunks on various vessels, tucked away out of sight. Still, this way they would get home alive, even though they might never shin up a jungle-giant again.

Given all this influx of visitors, it wasn't surprising that some old acquaintances turned up at the temple. One such was Captain Martan, the officer with whom I had conducted interrogations of prisoners – in another body, during another life.

As soon as I saw him, I wanted to grant him a private audience; but Donnah wouldn't allow it. With so many fighters infesting the place, my guards were in a high state of alert. During those days of the fleet's lay-over, a pile of weaponry often lay in the entry porch atop the purple stairway, confiscated from the 'jacks before they could enter my presence. Donnah ever kept her hand close to her pistol during audiences, while the other guards dangled best Guineamoy machetes behind their backs in addition to the daggers they wore in their belts. My women had little enough experience in wielding such – compared with the visiting soldiery! Maybe that was why the visitors regarded my armed guards so nonchalantly, by and large, and didn't take offence.

I had to hold my tettytet with Martan in public.

'You witnessed an important moment in my lives, Captain,' I said to him.

'You are She who has several lives.' Martan gave a practical kind of a nod, as though by the law of averages important moments were bound to crop up more often during the course of several lives, than during one; irrespective of how short they were. He sounded as though he was bestowing a title: She Who Has Several Lives.

'Do you recall that brute of a Son we questioned? The one who berserked?'

'How could I forget, little lady?' Oh, wasn't he the one for fine labels of a sudden! Or was he teasing? There seemed to be a twinkle in his eye. The Martan whom I remembered had been an honest, wholesome, realistic fellow, doing a dirty job as decently as possible. He hadn't been one for airs and graces, or hypocrisy.

So I grinned at him, and he grinned back.

'If we'd gone ahead and tormented that Son,' I said, 'we would have learned about Edrick for sure. He likely wouldn't have killed me. So none of what has happened would have happened.'

'Just as well we didn't torture him, eh?' Torture: he used the true word.

'It was you who tipped the balance, Martan.'

He looked surprised. 'Oh, I don't think so.'

'You told me you wouldn't want to be tortured yourself. That was a crossroads in my life. And even though Edrick got to torture *me* on the planet Earth – '

'*Where? He did what?*'

I lowered my voice. 'You'll have to wait for my next book, *The Book of the Stars*. And though he tortured me, I say, I still believe we made the right choice that day. I learnt a lesson from that. If we on this world wouldn't like our brains burnt out by the Godmind of Earth, neither would anybody else wherever they are, whether they're Sons of Adam or fishpeople of a far star. We've no right to save ourselves at their expense.'

He spoke softly too. 'What's this about burning people's brains?'

'Hush for now, Martan. Keep your ears open.'

He gazed at me a while, then nodded.

Among soldiers who have risked their lives together I suppose there's a comradeship beyond even that of a guild. I hadn't fought alongside Martan and his 'jacks, but we'd spent several weeks together at the prison pens; and thanks to that rabid Son's assault on us, I believe I shared a bond of comradeship. When Martan was departing, Donnah buttonholed him. I heard her demand to know what I'd whispered. 'Just giving me her private blessing, that's all,'

45

came Captain Martan's reply. He spoke loudly so that I would hear, and looked calmly across at me.

Another visitor whom I received later that same day was the acerbic 'Moustache', last encountered in the Jay-Jay Hall at Jangali.

This fellow wanted neither to bless me nor to receive my blessing. (Not that I'd been especially obsessed with 'blessing' people, until Martan came up with this excuse! I'd stoutly resisted having my hand slobbered on by ancient grannies, who were looking forward to reliving their gay young days in the *Ka*-store.)

Moustache's attitude to me hadn't changed. He sketched a parody of a bow.

'Thanks for the ride home, Trouble. Though no thanks for the walk to the war.'

'Welcome into the *Ka*-store,' I said. 'And may you not enter it too soon by tumbling out of a hoganny.'

'Never say that to a junglejack!' he growled back. 'It's ill luck.'

As with Martan, I lowered my voice. 'Don't you know yet? There's no such thing as ill luck for us any longer. There's only ill luck for everyone else in the galaxy.'

'Eh?'

'Talk to Captain Martan. Keep your ears open.'

Moustache had argued strenuously in council that the 'jacks should let Verrino go to rack and ruin just so long as Jangali, cordoned by jungles, was okay. 'What's Guineamoy to us?' he had said. He had been proved wrong.

'What's Earth to us, when we have our fortress of a *Ka*-store? What does Marl's world matter?' The same principle applied.

When my news of the stars broke, I hoped Moustache would make the connexion and be conscious of why I'd spoken. He was influential. He was my enemy (though

46

maybe that's too strong a term). And I was apparently impregnable. So why had I chosen to confide in him? This should make him wonder if all was quite as it seemed.

But I was about to relate the unexpected solution to my problem . . .

The 'jacks had already departed Pecawar a while since when the promised (or threatened) savant sailed in ex Ajelobo. Chanoose took time out to present him formally in my throne room.

Would he turn out to be a grim pedant? A smart pretentious spark, or what? I had no inkling – and didn't much care, either way. All I foresaw from him was nuisance; and who wants to brood on varieties of nuisance? (Well, some people do . . . I once knew one such aboard the *Speedy Snail*. Nuisance possessed that particular lady to the virtual exclusion of all else. Everything was a source of nuisance to her; including most of her riversisters, turn by turn. She squandered half of her life by inflaming herself at *this* nuisance, and railing at *that* nuisance. She provided an object lesson; and I hadn't allowed the prospect of our savant's arrival to sour one moment of my writing.)

His name was Stamno. He was of medium height and build, with receding fawn hair which was wispy and greasy (when I first met him). An unfortunate centre parting made it look as though someone had tried to saw his skull open. The surviving thatch, he wore longer than suited him; fraying oily curls lapped the nape of his neck. He must have been in his forties, yet his face was a very young one – so long as you ignored some deep criss-cross creases around his eyes. His manner was extremely courteous and attentive; unctuously so.

To anticipate somewhat: by that same evening he had washed his hair, which had been soiled by travel, and

47

during the course of his stay in the temple he must have repeated the treatment at least once every two days. He was a sort of sensual prude, if I can put it that way. He was the kind of person who would flirt but never actually fondle, as if he was holding himself in reserve . . . but for what? Perhaps in pursuit of some ideal. One day he would wake up and his life would have passed him by; meanwhile he wore a velvety maroon doublet and green hose, washed his locks obsessively, and spoke in consciously well-turned phrases.

'I'm delighted to acquaint myself with you, priestess!'

'And hullo to you.'

'Of any service I can be to you, only let me know.' Sometimes he tried to speak too cleverly. His phrases were so well turned that they turned head over heels. They tripped themselves up, instead of tripping off his tongue.

'I'll be sure to, Stamno.'

'Certain problems present themselves to me, which I hope you may be able to clarify. For instance . . .'

I listened to a string of *for instances* with mounting exasperation, though I didn't let this show.

'An exegesis is called for,' he concluded.

'A what?'

'An interpretation of your book; a commentary. Exposition. Or should we say – ' and he smirked ingratiatingly – 'of your books in the plural, since I understand that most happily you are busy upon – '

'Who's calling for a commentary?' I interrupted.

'Why, *The Book of the River* itself calls out; surely.'

Feel free! Comment away till you're blue in the face. And meantime, the Godmind gets ready to burn brains.

'Oh, piss off,' I muttered under my breath.

I think Stamno heard me; and this was the strangest thing, for his eyes seemed to light up gleefully. Pleased at being able to interfere with me? I thought not. Pleased, for some other reason . . .

'We do hope you'll co-operate with Savant Stamno,' said Chanoose.

'Who could resist it?' I said. 'But I'm sure Stamno wants to settle in right now.'

And Stamno smoothed his wayward, failing hair.

In the event Stamno didn't make himself too much of a nuisance, though he did keep on dropping convoluted hints about my work in progress. I tossed him a few sprats of information to chew on. He couldn't tell the guild anything they didn't already know.

Work on the dikes proceeded. I carried on writing, at speed, and was nearly at the end of the book. Tam continued crafting pots and bowls to be sold outside. Pilgrims persisted in calling; and preparations for the Grand Regatta came to a head. Once the regatta had seemed weeks away; all of a sudden the quays were crowded with vessels once more, and men from Verrino, Gangee and even Gate of the South were wandering around town. Not too many from Verrino. In the wake of looting and other ravages of war, maybe they couldn't scrape up the fare. The weather was hotting up.

Oh what a fine regatta it was, to be sure! Masts high, scraping the sky – flags and bright rags of bunting – a small orchestra on one deck, a flute and drum band on another! More fish-masks than I'd ever seen being sported by riversisters; it seemed as though the contents of the deep had hopped ashore. A conga-dance wormed along Pemba Avenue then all around town. Races were run up rigging to release bladders painted silver and red, inflated with watergas. And there was the marvel, as promised by Chanoose, of an enormous passenger balloon.

This balloon was a sphere, open at the bottom, buoyed up by hot air rising from a gas flame in the basket beneath. The basket was big enough to hold half a dozen people including the operator, with a fair-sized telescope for them to peer through. The flame was turned low every ten minutes and the balloon guided back down by its tether rope to allow as many brave spirits as possible to ascend. I need hardly add that the tether was essential, else the balloon would have departed on the breezes; which made me puzzle about the reliability of honeymoon flights. Apparently means of steering were under investigation.

And there was a parade – and a multitude of tasty snacks – and tipple a-plenty, not forgetting slugs of the black current which I doled out for hours from a tented pavilion erected on the waterfront. This was a bit of a bore. On the other hand I couldn't manage much real tippling on my own account. Spirit willing; body too young.

Nor could I participate in the other amusements except as spectator, for reasons of dignity, safety, short legs and such. I did at one stage beg childishly to be allowed to go up in the observation balloon; *not*, I hasten to add, out of any sudden urge to heed the Worm's suggestion and leap to my death. Donnah, ever nearby, put her foot down.

'If a lunatic slashed the rope, you'd drift away. We could lose you.'

Dad, who was sitting at a portable table noting names and addresses and keeping a tally of newly-enrolled devotees, nodded his entire agreement.

Round about the middle of the afternoon, Tam sidled up to me.

'Popped back to the temple,' he murmured. 'Found Stamno rifling your scritoire, reading what you've written. He'd picked Peli's lock.' In his hand he disclosed a strong wire with a little hook on the end.

'Chanoose put him up to it! While we're busy here! I bet she did.'

'No, no. That's where you're wrong. Guards didn't even try to delay me on the way in. Just nods and smiles from them. *They didn't know.* Stamno seemed scared I'd kick up an almighty barney, and they'd find out. Practically begged me to shut up.'

'That's odd. Are my papers safe?'

'Made him lock them up again.'

'Tonight, Tam, you and I will have a few words with Master Savant Stamno!'

We did indeed. And be damned how tired I was feeling after my day's activities. (Or inactivities.)

Peli was also present when Tam hustled Stamno into my chambers late that night. A single oil lamp burned. We seated Stamno near this so that his face was brightly lit, while ours were in the shadow. I noticed how Stamno had taken time out to wash his hair yet again.

'Well?' I said. 'Explain yourself, snooper.'

Stamno worried at a fingernail; though more as if he was manicuring it.

'With pleasure,' he said. 'I'm delighted to tell you. For you are not quite as you seem, any more than I am.'

'Aren't I, indeed?'

'You wish to save other worlds from the Godmind, not just ourselves. *How* this could be accomplished, you don't know. Nor do I. But you wish it.'

I nodded. 'Carry on.'

'Whereas the river guild want to sew this one world of ours up tight – irrespective of the Sons, irrespective of any other humans in the galaxy. Even irrespective of whether the Godmind might attain reality and truth, though the price be high.'

51

'You aren't rooting for the Godmind, surely!'

'No; I belong to the Guild of the Seekers of Truth.'

'Never heard of it.'

Stamno shrugged. 'If truth be hidden, let its seekers also be concealed.'

'Cutely put,' said Peli. 'Doesn't that boil down to your belonging to some nutty little cult consisting of about three members?'

Our savant pursed his lips. 'We have connexions with wise women in the Port Barbra hinterland.'

'You mean those sex fiends who orgasm for hours on a fungus drug?' I chipped in.

'Your information is distorted, Yaleen. That is only an aspect.' It was his first use of my name; hitherto he had only called me 'priestess'. Suddenly his voice was full of wonder, as though here at last was the ideal – the climax – for which he had preened and prepared himself, and withheld himself waiting, all his born days. 'To halt time itself, Yaleen! To perceive the Real beneath the flow of Phenomena! Why, *you* actually turned time back upon itself.'

'Sure I did. Which gives us a wee breathing space before most of the human race gets snuffed.'

'That too is important,' he acknowledged.

'You don't say.'

'Your new book won't be printed – not entire. Yet it *must* be. I'll tell you how. A copy has to be smuggled out.'

'Tell us something new,' said Peli. 'Those guards watch what goes out like snapperfish.'

'Merely a practical detail! First, we need a good copy. I shall make it. I pen quickly. Once my copy is clear away from here – '

'You'll send it straight to your crackpot Guild of Seekers,' Tam said suspiciously. 'And that'll be that.'

52

'No! Everybody must read it. Obviously it can't be printed here in Pecawar. It should be printed in Port Barbra.'

'Uh?' said Tam. 'No books are ever printed there. They don't know how.'

'Hear me out! That's an excellent reason for sending the copy there.'

'What, where it can't be printed?'

'Listen to me. All the type for Ajelobo's printing presses is made in Guineamoy. Likewise the type for newssheet presses everywhere. En route here, I stopped over at Guineamoy and made enquiries. I seek truth everywhere, you see! I assess all options. I discussed with a metalsmith the crafting of a special new fount of type – and the cost plus a price for discretion. We agreed; I commissioned the making of the fount.'

'You hadn't seen Yaleen's new book then,' said Peli. 'You're lying.'

'We Seekers, in Ajelobo and 'Barbra, wish to print pamphlets privately. Truth is about to blossom. Such changes recently!'

'Yon bunch of Seekers must have plenty of spare fish to toss around,' said Tam.

'In the past – how shall I put this without sounding coarse? – several prosperous patrons have appreciated the erotic aspect of our investigations.'

'And burned themselves up in the process, I'll be bound!' I said. 'I know about that drug. You're old by thirty if you over do it. So your Seekers are content to hook rich fools on early death, and buy printing type with the proceeds!'

Stamno's eyes gleamed. 'Never mind about that. The whole galaxy might die before its time. In any case I must dissociate the Seekers of Truth from some of the more carnal activities of our own associates – which are best regarded, mind you, as a mask, a guise, a Special Path.'

'Path where? To the graveyard?'

'You don't understand. Hear me out. The new type fount will be consigned to Port Barbra. Our associates have great influence over the newssheet in 'Barbra. Necessarily so! They don't want slanderous rumours published about them. *The Book of the Stars* will be printed in that newly minted typeface – untraceable! It will appear in the form of a flat newssheet of many pages. It won't be elegant and it won't be bound. The paper will be raggier. But it will be shipped everywhere covertly in that disguise – then released simultaneously. After which, you will publicly confirm your authorship.'

'If I'm allowed.'

'If you aren't, savants in Ajelobo will soon prove by exegesis that it is no forgery.'

The confrontation had got completely turned around; and in short order. I began to appreciate the cunning style in which Stamno must have inveigled his way into the good graces of the river guild over a number of years without any 'mistresses suspecting deceitful intent; all for the sake of his ideal. There was a lot about this set-up which I didn't like. But nevertheless . . . and nevertheless, again!

'Okay,' I said, 'we'll do it.'

'That's all very well,' said Peli, 'but how do we smuggle *Stamno's* copy out? I can't very well stuff the pages up my whatnot.' She nudged Stamno, embarrassing him.

'In pots!' exclaimed Tam. 'We'll smuggle it out a part at a time in pots with false bottoms. They're used to seeing me shift pots around, and take them out to the stall.'

'Where I'll ensure that they're snapped up promptly,' said Stamno. 'I'll employ an agent.'

54

'They're used to looking in my pots, too. That's where the false bottom comes in.'

'Forgive me if this is a dumb question,' said Peli, 'but won't the papers burn to a frazzle if you're baking a false bottom over them?'

'No. I'll put them in pots I've already made. I'll fold the sheets tight, wrap them in waxed paper, then tamp clay down on top. I'll just dry the false bottom by hanging the pot over a lamp; and I'll brush paint on to look like a glaze. The guards can peer inside to their heart's content. I'll make the necks of the pots too narrow to get their hands down.'

Two mornings later, there was a bustle on the river. All the regatta visitors were being packed off home again. (Incidentally, I'd hoped that Hasso might avail himself of the temporary liberty of the waterway to pay me a visit. No such luck; maybe he couldn't afford the fare.) In the midst of these manoeuvres, hoping that they provided a pretty distraction, I sought Donnah and requested a lot more paper.

'Why? Is the book turning out long?'

'Oh yes. Besides, I spoiled oodles of sheets.'

'That many? I hadn't noticed.'

'I threw them in the river, didn't I? I made paper boats.'

Donnah provided paper.

Stamno set to at his scribing task, working in his own cubby-hole of a room which he kept locked without causing comment, since he of course was a friend of the guild. Tam for his part began producing pitchers with narrow necks so that the guards would get used to seeing them. And I rushed to finish my writing.

Quite soon came the day when Chanoose called by to announce that work on the dikes would be completed the following Tauday. The 'jacks were almost home. The prisoners were safely beyond Aladalia, battened down, ready to be freighted over. Another few days, and the water could be pumped out of the dikes.

'What a fine success our regatta was,' she cooed at me.

'I couldn't agree more.' That was when we had uncovered Stamno and hatched our scheme.

'The number of visits here is falling off, though.'

'Yes, I'd noticed.' Thank goodness; I'd needed the extra hours.

'It's only to be expected. Price of success, eh? Do you know, we've enrolled almost the whole of Pecawar? Therefore the guild has decided that shortly you should go on a grand progress lasting half a year or so – down south to Tambimatu, first, then all the way north at least to Aladalia.'

'But . . . but Tam just came from Aladalia to be with me!'

'Not to worry! With all that expensively gotten clay in his hands, he ought to be as happy as a mud-hopper. You see, people *are* joining us in the other towns – but your presence on the spot will attract many more. We do want the maximum number safely in the fold before the Godmind attacks, don't we?'

'Yes,' I mumbled weakly.

'Good, that's all settled. You can set off on Rhoday next. Women only on the river by then!'

'Rhoday next, eh?' Stamno smoothed the hair lapping his nape. 'I've nearly caught up in my copying.'

'There's only a tiny bit more,' I said. 'I'm nearly done.'

'We'd better start smuggling tomorrow. Right, Tam?'

Tam was staring at me slack-jawed.

'Half a year or so! What does "or so" mean? Maybe

56

they'll decide you ought to tour the river permanently. In which case, why did I ever come here?'

'To make pitchers, that's why,' replied Stamno. 'Pitchers in which to hide paper.'

Tam bunched those bony fists of his; for once in his life he looked on the point of striking someone.

'I'll stick by your side,' Peli promised me. 'You can count on it.'

This only made matters worse; Tam smashed his fists together. He pounded his knuckles.

'Stow it!' snapped Stamno. 'I don't see this as an ultimate tragedy. If need be, you can always walk home.'

'After all this effort they've put into getting the right clay for me, who says as I'll be allowed?'

Stamno disregarded this. 'If Yaleen's well away from here when *The Book of the Stars* appears, and if the river guild get vengeful, and if she happens to be in the general area of Ajelobo or Port Barbra – we Seekers can offer sanctuary.'

'I can hide in the forests and be the pet of your cult? Lovely, charming! Just what do you think the guild would do for revenge? Cut my head off?'

Stamno laughed in a dry, rattly way. 'We're wasting time in idle speculation. Fact number one: Yaleen is going on a trip. Fact number two: we have work to finish.'

'Just a mo,' said Peli. 'What are you going to be doing after Rhoday next, Stamno?'

'Me? I'll remain here in all innocence and study the writings which Yaleen leaves behind. What else? Thus Tam shall not be entirely bereft of congenial company.'

Was this some essay at humour?

Tam, bless him, grinned crookedly. 'With Peli gone off sailing, I could use another pair of hands at the kiln!'

'Oh dear me,' said Stamno.

'I hear you're going away,' said Mum. 'I think I shall come with you.'

'What? How about Dad? He can't sail. He's stuck here, same as Tam.'

'*I'm* not stuck.'

For a brief moment I almost hated my mother.

'Your father will be happy with his facts and figures,' she continued lightly. 'Temple statistics matter more than his spice accounts of old. Though of course those were also important; in their way.' Her voice hardened. 'I don't have a home any more, except with you, Yaleen. Do you suggest I remain as caretaker of an empty temple? A sort of human dust-sheet?'

'This temple won't be a ghost when I'm gone! If you think so, what price Dad's facts and figures – not to mention his happiness?'

She shrugged. 'This trip is different from your other trips, daughter dear. This time you won't be a young woman well able to look after yourself. You're only three years old.'

'Peli will be going.'

'Is Peli your *mother*?'

'She's a riverwoman! Um, maybe you and Dad ought to move back to our house while I'm away?'

'And caretake there, for a change? No, Yaleen, I want more. I have a right. Didn't I endure childbirth twice for you?'

'Yes, yes. But look, I really don't see how you can do this to Dad.'

'What am I doing?'

'Abandoning him, damn it!'

'Yet it's all right for me to be abandoned?'

'You wouldn't be. You'd be together.'

'Since I moved in here, Yaleen, I've become a person of some import. That's a new sensation for me. Your father and I spent years cosseted together. Narya's birth reaffirmed our ties – but it was a false reaffirmation, wasn't it?'

'Have you spoken to Dad about this?'

She shook her head. 'Not yet. I thought I'd tell you first. It's my decision, mine alone.'

'Mum, this trip mightn't be plain sailing.'

'Why ever not? Are we boarding a leaky boat?'

'Life's uncertain. Anything might happen.'

'Equally, anything might *not* happen. We'll just be away half a year, you and I.'

'Really made your mind up, haven't you?'

'High time, too! Others have been arranging my life for long enough. You, Chanoose, the guild. Yes, it's time to assert myself – just as you have always done. The mother learns from the daughter.' Mum smiled benevolently; it was such a smile as I had seen on Chanoose's face.

'Assert? I don't know that I've been in much of a position to do that lately.'

'Opinions might vary on that score. People seem to be forever running errands for you. All the way from Aladalia and Ajelobo. Building dikes, goodness knows what else. Now let's do something for *my* benefit, shall we? In turn I can help you assert yourself more effectively.'

This business has all gone to your head, I thought to myself. *You've become a dowager, from out of a story book . . .*

Again, that smile. 'Do you know, daughter, I haven't travelled anywhere significant since my wanderweeks all those years ago. *Now* I shall.'

'But . . .' *But I don't want you on that boat. I'm not really a child. Your presence will make me into one! You'll diminish me. You'll elbow out Peli who's my true ally.*

I couldn't bring myself to say any of this. She was my mother, after all. My mum twice over.

It was early on a Newday morning. In just twenty-four hours we were due to sail – me, Mum, Peli, Donnah, and assorted guards – aboard a schooner, the *Crackerjill*, which had been placed entirely at our disposal. First port of call: Gangee.

Almost the whole of Stamno's copy of *The Book of the Stars* had already been smuggled out of the temple at the bottom of various pitchers. The previous evening, I had finished the last few pages – for Stamno to copy, and Tam to encase in clay. The job would have been completed overnight.

I was sitting on the top step of the marble stairway which led down to Pemba Avenue. I was hugging my knees as I watched the world go by to work. Quite a few people waved to me; I smiled and ducked my head at them. Guardswoman Bartha loitered a few paces behind, keeping an eye.

I heard voices from the entry hall: Tam's – and Mela's. Mela was another guard.

'Let's have a look, then,' she was saying.

'Oh, you've seen the like of these before.' Tam sounded perfectly casual.

I looked round. He had one pitcher in his hand and another tucked under his arm.

'Just so,' said Mela. 'I've been thinking how that style's rather ugly for a hot-shot potter – specially now that you have the super clay to make true porcelain.'

'I've had to keep my hand in.'

'You couldn't even get a hand in one of those. How do you clean it? I wouldn't buy a jug I couldn't clean.'

'It isn't a jug. It's a pitcher. You just swill it out.'

'Yet most days lately I've seen you take a couple of those down to yon stall; where they certainly don't gather dust. They're grabbed almost before you can say *Ka*-store.'

'That's gratifying to hear.'

'Oh, didn't you *know*?'

I didn't dare continue watching, in case I seemed anxious. Perhaps it was time to arrange a little diversion? Such as Yaleen tumbling downstairs?

'Let's take a closer look at these much-desired items, shall we?'

I heard fumbling, stamping – then a splintering crash. 'Oh *shit*!' cried Tam.

I jerked round. The pitcher from under his arm lay shattered.

'Look what you've gone and done!' he bellowed. But he didn't sound panicked.

'That's exactly what I'm doing: looking.' Mela toed the fragments with her boot, sorting them about.

Ah. The broken pitcher had been a decoy. Tam had dropped it deliberately.

I jumped up. 'Hey, you! Mela!'

Bartha clamped a hand on my shoulder, suppressing me.

'Now let's break the *other* one,' suggested Mela silkily.

'Oh come on,' growled Tam. 'What do you think you're playing at?' But his cheeks had flushed.

'Guild security,' said Mela. She snatched at the pitcher in his hand. Tam jerked it away. She grabbed again. He swung it high out of reach.

Then the incredible happened. To extend her reach, Mela unsheathed her machete and slashed at the pitcher. The target clove in half, leaving Tam clutching the neck.

61

The base flew away in my direction, smashing on the floor. Potsherds lay scattered – and amidst them a slab of uncooked clay, with an edge of waxed paper sticking out. Bartha's hand became a vice on my shoulder.

'What's *that*?' exulted Mela.

Tam lost his cool. Discarding the top of the pitcher he dived to secure the waxed package. Mela also dived. The machete, which was still in her hand, was a part of her hand. It was the reach she lacked. As Tam's fingers closed around the clay-wadded paper, Mela's hand descended fiercely. The machete blade chopped Tam's wrist and stuck in the floor.

Pulsing squirts of blood spouted – over a hand which lay severed. Tam's blood was pumping from a stump. Mela's machete had sliced right through flesh, muscle and bone.

Tam didn't howl. Maybe he couldn't feel any pain yet. Maybe the pain was blotted out by the sight before his eyes. He lay sprawled, staring madly at his potter's right hand – and his wrist-stump spurting life-blood.

Mela sprawled too. She still held her weapon, with the edge buried like a cleaver in a butcher's block. Her teeth were chattering crazily.

No, Tam didn't howl. But I did. And what I was howling was, 'Current! Current! Madden Mela! Kill her! Send her to the Earth!'

No such thing happened. The Worm didn't rear itself in Mela's mind. (And maybe this was just as well. Who wants a priestess who can frenzy you and slay you when she fancies, with a chant of hatred?) Nor did my frantic wrenching release me from Bartha's grasp. But my cries alerted the temple. Feet came running.

Donnah took in the scene in a trice. 'Tourniquet!' she screamed. Tearing her own belt free, she ripped Tam's sleeve away and began binding the belt above his elbow.

'Another one! Wads! Bandage!' Within moments Donnah was tightening somebody else's belt just below Tam's shoulder. I'd run out of breath to howl by now – and he, I think, had fainted. 'Salve! And clay! Wet clay to plaster on!'

Presently Donnah rose. Mela hovered nearby, brandishing the waxed package. Her blade stayed stuck in the floor. She thrust her discovery at Donnah.

'Here! He was trying to sneak this out. It was buried in clay at the bottom of the jug. When the jug got smashed he tried to snatch it. He would have run off with it. So I had to . . . It was an accident, Donnah: his hand. I swear it.'

Donnah accepted the package. She ripped it open, unfolded the sheets written in Stamno's hand and scanned them. 'So,' she said.

'It was an accident.' Mela's voice pleaded. 'That thing's important, isn't it?'

'Yes. But you . . . exceeded all bounds. And in front of *her*! Get out of my sight, Mela!'

Mela fled.

A wide board from a trestle table was brought. Tam was eased on to this. By now he was moaning and shivering. Tremors racked his body. Two guards bore him away, within.

Donnah approached me slowly, and knelt to be on a level with me. 'I think we've saved him, Yaleen.'

'Saved him?' I cried in her face. 'You've destroyed him! He's a potter without a hand! You might as well kill him, and be done. Let him go to the *Ka*-store. That's the only place where he can be a potter now – the potter of his memories!'

'With good care, he'll be well.' Her face twisted. 'He'd better be. I have questions to ask – him, and Savant

Stamno. I shan't bother you with such questions, my priestess. You have much to occupy your mind, with the *Crackerjill* due to sail.' She was controlling herself only with difficulty. She was trembling. She was scared. Of Chanoose's reaction to the news of this obscene mutilation? Or of her rage at *why* it had occurred?

'I'm not sailing anywhere, you stupid sow! You pissing stinger!'

'Tam will be most courteously looked after. I swear by *The Book*! I do realize what he means to you, Yaleen. We may even be able to fit him with some sort of spatula on the end of his wrist.'

'A spatula? Why not just nail a shovel-head on him!'

'Reports of his progress will be flashed to you faithfully. Mela will be punished. She'll be kicked out of the temple. Right out of the guild! I promise you she'll never sail again. But *you* must sail, Yaleen – for everybody's sake.'

To my astonishment I saw that she was weeping. She put an arm around my shoulder and hugged me tenderly. Her salt tears were on my cheeks. I was so surprised that I didn't spit or hiss or bite her.

I felt my own eyes watering, and a moment later I was sobbing – just like the kid I looked to be. Peli wasn't there to comfort me. But I knew that I couldn't have surrendered to Peli in the way that I now surrendered to Donnah – because Peli was my comrade. Nor with my mum could I have broken down. Yet with Donnah suddenly it was possible. Why so? Was it because I had betrayed Donnah; and now found myself comforting her just as much as she was comforting me?

'I'm still not going,' I sniffled into her red hair.

'If you don't want to, little one,' she murmured, 'your boat can wait. We can wait. The whole world can wait.'

Which, of course, meant that I would have to sail as

planned. No world can wait. Neither ours, nor all the others.

'Yaleen!' It was Dad's voice.

'Donnah,' I whispered, 'I only did what I did for the best, without malice.' Gently I detached myself from her embrace; gently she let me do so.

'Of course you did,' she murmured back. Sad? Scared? I no longer knew.

'Yaleen.' Dad strode across the hall, skirting the blood-puddles and the machete. 'I just heard about Tam. It's terrible. Awful. The poor lad! I promise I'll care for him. I shan't let him despair. I'll help him be whole again – in spirit at least.'

'Thanks, Dad. But I *am* sailing tomorrow. You needn't worry on that score.'

His look showed that I had wounded him. But he merely said, 'Look after your mother for me, will you? Whilst I'm looking after Tam?'

'If I can, Dad. If I can. It isn't always easy to look after people – when they have the wind in their sails.'

'Don't I know it,' I heard Donnah say softly.

We were all being very delicate and tender with each other. We were all hurt equally, and we had enough strength to wallow in our hurt. Unlike Tam, whose wound was the worst. The most unendurable.

Tam's condition was stable by the evening. He wasn't going to die. He wasn't going to lose the rest of his arm to gangrene. The tourniquets had been removed.

Stamno had vanished. Nobody could find him – and no one had seen him go out that morning. So presumably he hadn't been lurking along Pemba Avenue waiting for his agent to acquire the last pitcher from the arcade. He must have heard the commotion – and somehow decamped, over the yard wall, though I would have thought that impossible, and him not much of an athlete to look at. Clearly the threat to his quest had driven him to some desperate exertion.

Or had he contrived to slip out earlier on? Had he been intending to decamp in any case – contrary to what he had told me – just as soon as he laid hands on the last sheets? I didn't know.

I certainly didn't volunteer any information about Stamno, to a most displeased Chanoose. I didn't breathe a word about the type-makers of Guineamoy, or the Seekers of Truth, or the Port Barbra cult women.

Chanoose walked off with my own original copy of *The Book of the Stars*. Actually, I presented this to her before she could confiscate it. The book had ruined Tam; *I* didn't want it any more. Not that particular manuscript. And the copy, wherever it was, was only missing a few last pages of no great moment; in retrospect, of very little moment indeed.

The next morning I bade an awkward farewell to Tam. He lay in his room looking ashen – and so alone, though my father sat by him.

He did bring himself to say, 'I always had too many bones, Yaleen. Always, didn't I?' I didn't know whether he spoke bravely, or dementedly. Nor did I want to decide. I kissed him on the brow and fled upstairs – whence I was conveyed ceremonially to the quayside, perched in my seat strapped to poles.

We boarded: guards and Peli and Mum and me. Donnah too – my travelling major-domo now. Donnah looked mightily relieved to be sailing forth again. Yet until we actually cast off, she often glanced ashore as though

Chanoose might decide at this last and cruellest moment to replace her.

It was bright and breezy that Rhoday morn, though the sun would blaze hard by noon. Out on the waters the air smelled hopeful and healthy. Presently I spied the first of Tam's dikes. At that distance from shore I could barely make it out: just a thin line fringing the river, with a rude hut nearby for the watchman to occupy.

I imagined water being allowed to seep back to cover the exposed clay during the long weeks to come.

I hurried to find Donnah. I told her to send a signal back to Chanoose insisting that both dikes should be kept drained even if Tam looked like never crafting another pot in his life. Even if Tam *demanded* that they flood the beds of clay. Even if he quit Pecawar to walk home.

But nobody else should ever use that clay.

PART TWO

A Chef at the Palace of Enchantment

When we arrived in Guineamoy the town seemed even dirtier and smellier than last time I'd visited the place. The war had stimulated industry and with the coming of peace the host of manufacturers pursued the old avenue of profit with renewed vigour and capital, meanwhile searching out new ones too, for their rejigged workshops to supply.

Fresh advances in forging and metallurgy had occurred. New chemicals had been cooked up, and mixed in novel combinations (original object: combustion, explosions). Gases were being extracted from coals and other sorts of rock. Experiments were afoot.

More especially experiments were in the air – that was where you could sniff them. And spy them, too. Guineamoy was the home of the balloon which had graced our grand regatta. During our stay another hot-air balloon was undergoing trials. This specimen had wooden 'fans' jutting from its passenger basket. Powered by compressed air, these fans swished round to steer the balloon – slowly, by and large – against the breeze. Yet this method of steering couldn't have been too reliable. One day I saw the balloon drifting through the smoky sky without fans turning, heading towards the river. All of a sudden the flicker of fire and shimmer of air above the basket disappeared and the balloon was dropping fast. Before the craft could crash into the ground, the flame leapt briefly alive to buoy it up – and a rope with an anchor on the end was tossed out, its hooks snagging on a roof below.

However, the kind of industry I was interested in was

type-founding. Whilst I was presiding over what had come to be called 'communion' with the Worm – the solemn drinking of swigs of the black current – Peli was busy in town doing a spot of investigating. (I suppose I was in town too. But only just. Since men couldn't board the *Crackerjill*, a pavilion had been erected for me on the quayside; just as at Gangee and Gate of the South.)

I'd tried without success to deter Peli from aping a Port Barbra accent – the quiet murmur, the softly hooded consonants – as subterfuge. If she got excited she couldn't keep this up; and besides it was Stamno who had commissioned the new type fount, not some woman of 'Barbra. (Or so, at least, Stamno had told us.) But Peli liked the idea of disguising herself. She went equipped with a long scarf to wind round her head as a 'Barbra-style hood and mouth-mask while she was prowling the streets of Guineamoy. I'm sure this must have made her stick out like a sore thumb. It was high summer by the time we arrived. The heat wasn't so fierce or the air as humid as in the deep south, but the atmosphere was still pretty stifling. The sun was hazed with an overcast of smoke which pressed the hot exhalations of smelters back down to earth to add to the season's natural warmth.

True, a few of the locals had taken to wearing thin muslin masks to keep the smuts out of their nostrils; and coifs or snoods, besides, to protect their hair. Yet these eccentrics were strictly a minority. Judging by glances directed askance at such, not everybody in Guineamoy admired this new fashion. *Proper* Guineamoy folk should obviously suck the dirty air in with relish. They should stick a finger up their snouts and lick the grime. Undeterred, Peli sallied forth with six spans of wool to wrap about her countenance.

Wool was also wrapped around the whereabouts of the

metalsmith with whom Stamno claimed he had struck his secret deal. I had no special reason to think that Stamno had been lying, but in view of our savant's disappearance it seemed as wise to check up; and for a whole week Peli drew a blank.

She slipped into my cabin on the evening of that day when I saw the balloon make its emergency descent. She was muffled up to the gills.

'Peli, you nitwit! Do you want the whole boat to see you sneaking round like that?'

A chuckle issued from the scarf as she unwound it. She was grinning mischievously. 'Never fear: I just bundled up right outside the door. Figured a dramatic entry might be in order. Because . . . I found out!'

'You did?'

'Absolutely. Today I went over to Ferramy Ward. That's out towards the lake of filth. Town's expanding that way apace, Worm knows why, though I reckon some bright sparks must have found a way to use the liquid spoils. I spotted big barges with bucket chains tethered to buoys on the lake; not that I got right up to it, seeing as Ferramy Ward's already enough of a jungle of workshops and whatnots – '

'Yes, yes, but what *happened*?'

'Well, I used diligent guile. I didn't make myself conspicuous by asking leading questions. I found the fellow by a process of elimination. His name's Harrup, and his little factory was thumping away like a heart in love, stamping out this and that in hot metals, with balls of steam puffing out of the ventilators as if it was breathing . . .

'Anyway, I made out I was from 'Barbra, taking passage home aboard this *Crackerjill* of ours. That's just in case Harrup turns up here for his slug of darkness and spots me on board and wonders. I pretended Stamno was acting as

73

our agent – us being the 'Barbra mob – and how we were concerned in case he'd run off with our funds, seeing as we hadn't heard from him since. This was to winkle out whether Harrup has heard from him lately; and he hasn't. So anyhow, Harrup protested that he'd already consigned the new fount of type to 'Barbra a fortnight ago. This was a bit of an awkward moment, since it turns out that Stamno only paid Harrup half of the price in advance, and now Harrup wanted the rest – from *me*. But I said we'd only pay up when delivery was confirmed. Do you know how Stamno paid?'

'Cash?'

'No, diamonds. Lots of little sparklers from Tambimatu. Well, they don't really sparkle much, that sort, but it seems they've a use for them here on the tips of drills. So as diamonds go, they're poor specimens. But they aren't exactly cheap. Nor was the job.'

'So it's all true. That's a relief. Now we just have to hope that Stamno got the copy off safely.'

'He'd have been wise to walk to Gangee or Verrino first. The guild could have been searching all cargoes ex Pecawar.'

'I'm sure he'd have thought of that. But listen, Peli: you say he paid in Tambimatu diamonds. How did he get them?'

'From the cult women? He said they batten on rich patrons.'

'Yes, but wealth in 'Barbra means costly woods.'

'He could hardly carry a couple of cords of rubyvein around with him.'

'Hmm, and I doubt you need diamonds to drill holes in ivorybone. So why and whence the sparklers? *I* think there must be cultists, or at least Seekers for Truth, in Tambimatu too.'

74

'That figures. I prised a name out of Harrup, without him suspecting as I didn't know it. It's the name of the woman he sent the fount to in 'Barbra. She's called Peera-pa.'

'So?'

'So it's a Tambimatu name. When I was hunting round Tambimatu town for that bangle of mine – the coiled one, remember? – I noticed a name just like hers painted up over a lapidary's. Peera-sto; that was it. Odd name; stuck in me mind.'

'It could equally be a 'Barbra name.'

'So it could. But there's an obvious connexion. Funny things fester in deep-south jungles, Yaleen, and spread like sprintweed.'

Just then we heard a cursory knock on the door, and before either of us could react Donnah strode in. She held a letter in her hand.

'For you, Yaleen. Compliments of the quaymistress. It's from your father. There's one for your mother too.'

Ah, the post had caught up with us. Hitherto I'd had to rely on signals from Chanoose, attesting to Tam's well-being; whether true or false.

Donnah waited. So did I, till she went. Then I tore the letter open.

Dad confirmed that Tam was okay in body, and reasonably so in spirit too. He had declined Chanoose's fatuous offer to fix a wooden spatula on his stump, so that he could shape clay. One night Tam had wept in Dad's arms; though I wasn't ever to let Tam know that I knew this. The tears seemed to have flushed the poison from his soul. On the very next day he had gone to the dikes, with Dad accompanying him. As I read this letter I realized that Tam was fast becoming the son whom Dad had lost in Capsi. Together they brought back tubs of clay on a cart.

Tam, the one-handed potter, set to work again. However, he was no longer working with his kick-wheel. Instead – slowly and patiently, often cursing humorously – he was modelling porcelain *hands*. Hands reaching up. Hands holding fleuradieu blooms. Hitherto all of Tam's hands had proved to be abortions. Yet he insisted that he was going to craft the perfect porcelain hand, one which would blush like flesh and seem to come alive at night by lamplight.

Dad thought this was a healthy, creative response. I wasn't so sure, though I tried to believe it.

I mustn't have succeeded. That night I dreamed of the noon when Tam had arrived in Pecawar. In the dream I was waiting to meet him fresh off the *Merry Mandolin*. But when he strode down the gangplank towards me (minus any bags) the hand which he held out in greeting was a porcelain one, fused to his wrist of flesh and bone. The moment I clasped his hand, it cracked into a dozen pieces which fell tinkling to the flagstones of the quay.

We tarried four full weeks in Guineamoy. The reason was that in Guineamoy people seemed generally less eager to partake of the current and gain their ticket to the *Ka*-store than had been the case in Gangee or Gate of the South. A fair number did, to be sure. But the majority ignored us. And that would be their folly.

The Guineamoy quaymistress ascribed this reluctance to the prevailing ethic of practical utility, self-help, faith in tangible things. For instance, most metal equipment used on boats – such as anchors, rope-rings, winches, pumps – was manufactured in Guineamoy. Now in reality Guineamoy depended upon the river for its exports, but local wisdom held it that all river business hinged on Guineamoy skills. Thus men of Guineamoy weren't going to drink from the 'oil-pipe' of the current (as some local wits described it) any more than they would consider lapping bilge water.

This worried the river guild, on account of all the skills which would be lost if most smiths had their minds fried; which is why we lingered till visitors fell off to a mere dribble. Then we cried quits.

We stopped over at Spanglestream a single week; likewise at the Bayou. In both places our reception was everything we'd hoped for.

So, not long after, we were tying up at the massive natural stone quays of Jangali.

Of our stay in Jangali, the outstanding feature which I must mention is the conduct of my mum; and of that acid old acquaintance whom hitherto I have called 'Moustache' – but who naturally had a name of his own, to wit Petrovy.

The catalyst between Mum and Petrovy ('catalyst' being a term I had picked up in Guineamoy) was none other than dusky Lalo. You may recall Lalo – and her fiancé Kish – as the two who took passage home to Jangali aboard the *Spry Goose*, and who raised the alarm while I was rescuing the drugged Marcialla from her perch. Then a year later I had found myself pitying Kish because Lalo's mum was so thoroughly overbearing.

On our second morning in Jangali Lalo turned up in our reception marquee on the quayside. She was hanging on the arm of Moustache (whom I shall call Petrovy from now on), and at first I must admit I didn't recognize her, though I noticed Petrovy soon enough.

I was doing the honours, while Lana kept me supplied with constant refills of the current and Mum established some order among the throng of applicants.

A throng it was! – and Petrovy, with that young woman on his arm, didn't press forward right away but hung back for ages observing me. As the crowd thinned, Mum tried to usher them forward. Instead of heeding Mum's urgings, the young woman began chatting to her. Petrovy joined in, grumpily at first – so it looked to me – but soon with an increasing show of chivalry.

Now, that young woman was slim, wiry, taut and muscular. *I* would have expected Lalo to flesh out in the period which had elapsed since last I saw her. She'd become a mother. She had settled down, and under the aegis of a stoutly complacent parent who wished her to have at least three children in quick succession. I also recalled Lalo's crack about how the fungus drug didn't make sex any more thrilling. At the time she had spoken chirpily and innocently enough, but I remember suspecting a certain – shall we say? – undertone to her remark. If that note had become dominant, I shouldn't have been surprised if Lalo's initial interest in exciting Kish might not have gone to seed; along with the tone of her body.

Anyway, in the end Mum did bring Petrovy and the woman forward. Almost everyone else had gone by now, and no new arrivals were being admitted; it was almost lunchtime.

'I believe you know these two of old,' said Mum. 'I present Petrovy – and Lalo.'

'Lalo!' I cried, connecting at last.

'Why yes.' The lithe dusky woman executed a full turn – as if to show off a fine costume. Actually she was wearing a faded, stained scarlet blouse and baggy breeches tucked into fork-toed boots.

And then I made the full connexion and realized that she was indeed showing off her duds – her *work* clothes – as well as her new tougher leaner self inside them.

'You've become a junglejack! During the war, while the men were away – of course!'

'And after the war; and for a long while yet. I'm enjoying it. It's fun. I might possibly quit in ten years' time.' She squeezed Petrovy's arm. He uttered a *hrumph*.

'We always did have a few women junglejacks,' she added. 'Now we have a lot more.'

Hrumph again. Petrovy sounded resigned. 'We lost a fair number of guildsmen in the fighting. Lalo here has become quite an organizer. She's on the Council. She's shot up to the top of the hoganny tree faster than a cowchuck ball.'

'Amazing,' I said. 'And how about Kish?'

'Oh, he's happy enough looking after our kid.' Kid, singular. Obviously the grandmotherly ambitions of Lalo's mum hadn't come to fruition quite so quickly. Even so, Kish seemed to be a loser either way – unless he truly didn't mind.

'Nothing wrong there,' said Lalo, perhaps reading my look. 'Me, I'm jungle born and bred. Be cruel to send Kish up a tree. Remember how we joshed him about it? Kish and I discussed this, of course.'

No doubt they did. Presumably, though, Kish didn't need to feel jealous of Petrovy into the bargain. By hanging on the older junglejack's arm Lalo was mainly emphasizing a professional relationship – rubbing and squeezing it home, no less. Presumably.

Just then Petrovy did detach himself from Lalo, gently but firmly. Turning to Mum he said, with a bob of his head, 'Madam, I should be delighted if you would accept my hospitality in town. Here in Jangali we have a fine local watering-hole, by name – '

'The Jingle-Jangle,' Mum nodded. 'I've read of it.'

'May I assure you that it isn't too rowdy during the day?'

Mum's eyes gleamed; and in that gleam I saw that she

was determined to recapitulate my own adventures. 'I'd be delighted,' she said.

'Perhaps Lalo and Yaleen would prefer to mull over old times,' suggested Petrovy.

'Whilst *we* mull something else! Ah, but you don't mull junglejack. I'm mixing my drinks!'

Petrovy grinned. 'Mustn't do that.'

'Oh I can't stop,' breezed Lalo, 'much as I'd like to. I have trees to shin up this afternoon. And as to booze, a shot of the black current will suit me fine for now.'

This was duly provided. Whereupon Lalo departed, giving me a cheery smile – followed in short order by Mum, who had taken Lalo's place on Petrovy's arm. Which left me to wonder: *What is Petrovy up to?*

As soon as I got back on board I had an urgent word with Peli. 'Peli dear, would you mind going to the Jingle-Jangle right away?'

'Just try to stop me!'

'Mum's gone off there with that 'jack I told you about: the one with the moustaches.'

'The big-shot you hinted things to?'

'The same. His name's Petrovy. I want to know what his game is. Can you keep an eye on them both from a distance?'

'I'll wear my scarf. They won't spot me.'

Peli didn't report back till nightfall, which was a good while after Mum herself had returned on board.

'Well?'

'That's exactly how they got on! Well indeed. Your mum and Petrovy spent two solid hours in the Jingle-Jangle. They didn't drink immoderately, but by the time they left they were into quite a tettytet. Oh they were brushing against each other every few minutes accidentally on purpose in the way of two people who have every intention of, well . . .'

'I get the picture.'

'So then Petrovy escorted your mum back to his own house. Leastways I'm assuming it was his, and not just borrowed for the occasion. To get there you head past the Jay-Jay Hall then turn right down Whittlers Alley then – '

'I'm not planning a visit, Peli. What happened?'

'They stayed together around three hours. Then your mum left, on her own; and I hung around to see whether Petrovy would rush off anywhere. But he didn't; and that's why I'm back late. It wasn't the sort of place you could sneak up and peep into. It's the second storey up a jacktree, so I don't actually know what went on inside.'

'But we assume they went to bed.'

Peli scratched her head. 'They must have done, I'd say. Your mum's hair was astray when she came out, and she had a certain look on her face. Cat and cream, cat and cream.'

'You must have watched for ages.'

'Oh, I've stood watch on a boat. It's no different on dry land, except you have to watch out for people spotting you. Bit tiresome, that's all.'

'Hmm. I wonder how tired Mum's feeling?'

'She didn't look the least bit tired.'

Next morning I arranged to have breakfast with Mum, just the two of us alone together.

'So what did you make of Petrovy?' I asked over a waffle. 'He's a vigorous sparring partner. Er, in debate, I mean.'

She looked me right in the eye. 'Whereas your dad has always been so gentle, eh? That's what's nice about your father. But one man isn't all men, Yaleen. And of course I'm no-one's fool, either – so whenever my new friend ventured queries about a certain surprise which priestess Yaleen might have in store, I found more interesting business to occupy us. If he was keeping his ears open, I plugged them with my tongue. Figuratively, of course.'

'Of course, Mum.'

'Not that I have any inkling what this certain surprise might be! Nor how Petrovy has any inkling of it – though I must say he seemed sympathetic. To it; and to me. Thankfully, my inevitable reticence on this point,' and here she chose her words very carefully, 'did not put a strain on his courtesy. Had it done so, I should have felt rather disappointed in him. I might have suspected that he was paying court to the daughter through the mother. That would have been quite galling, don't you think?'

'I'm glad to hear you enjoyed yourself.'

'Oh I did. I enjoyed being with him. Though since there was apparently a hidden motive, I think I shall not repeat the experience. That might prove boring.'

Oh dear. Mum had had time to mull over the events of the previous afternoon and see those in a new light – one to which, despite her insistence, she had perhaps been blind at the time. And she blamed me. I had robbed her tryst with Petrovy of a certain precious spontaneity.

'Incidentally,' she added, 'I did notice your Peli lurking in the Jingle-Jangle. She isn't always enormously subtle.'

Oh double dear. 'Look on the bright side, Mum. If Petrovy *hadn't* wanted something – '

'Then he wouldn't have wanted me? Charming.'

'No, what I mean is . . .' I trailed off. I was only putting my foot further in my mouth.

Mum patted my hand. 'Never mind, Yaleen. A mature

woman can set aside a smidgeon of subterfuge, from the meat of the affair.'

'Oh. Good.'

'How fascinating if I knew what your little surprise might be! I imagine Peli knows.'

'Uh,' I grunted, and concentrated on waffle.

I related all this to Peli to caution her. Thus it was with great glee that she in turn related to me, two nights later, how Petrovy had just happened to bump into her in town that day, and how he had whisked her off to the Jingle-Jangle. Obviously Petrovy hadn't spotted Peli spying on his courtship of Mum.

'So I says to myself,' said Peli, 'if your mum can enjoy herself, why shouldn't *I*? Not that I'd ever dream of putting her nose out of joint by letting on! Anyhow, I did bear in mind that I wasn't supposed to know the way to that house of his. Wouldn't have done if I'd charged hot-foot ahead through every twist and turn, would it now?'

I giggled. Yet in fact – would you believe? – I was starting to experience a twinge of jealousy at these amusements in which I couldn't participate. Truth to tell, I was feeling a tad frustrated. Not that I could have imagined amusing myself with Petrovy, of all people! On the other hand, Peli with her bluff red face and her hair like a haystook, wasn't as, well, attractive as I'd once been . . . (Unworthy thoughts! That's what a pang of jealousy does to people.)

'So when we got back to his house up the tree, we please ourselves; and I shan't go into that. But while I was feeling, um, relaxed he started hinting on about the little surprise. "I don't want to tease you, Pet," I said to him. He didn't seem to mind me calling him Pet. "I'll tell you the truth," said I. Seeing as your mum said he appeared to be sympathetic – '

'Hey, Mum might just have said that so that if Petrovy found out, he'd tell her; and she could tell Donnah!'

'Your mum said she wasn't going to see him again. But that's by the by. I'm no one's fool, either. What I told him was this: "There's a surprise all right, Pet, but it'll have to stay hush for the moment. If the river guild hears about it . . . you follow?"

'"*I'm* not river guild," says he.

'"Ah, but you don't always know who you're talking to," I said.

'He seemed a bit offended. "Don't I just?"

'"No," I answered him. "For instance you've been talking to Yaleen's mum – and *she* doesn't necessarily see eye to eye with Yaleen." That took the wind out of his sails, all right – as well as serving to caution him.

'"You wily old fox," he calls me. But I gave him a cuddle to make up. "Foxes are legends," I said, "but there'll be real foxes somewhere else in the galaxy – and lots of other people, who are just as real as you and me. Be a shame to lose them all forever, now wouldn't it be? All those deaths would diminish us – and the river guild would be the one big fish forever after, monopolizing *Ka*-store and everything."

'"That's not on," he says, "not after all we've fought for. Though mind you, I do believe in the *Ka*-store."

'"But you don't want to pay *too* high a price for the privilege," I put it bluntly.

'He frowns at me. "Look, Peli, our different towns and guilds have always had a lot of independence. Happen we've had to rely on one particular guild to link us all up, but still the river guild couldn't rule us. That's what bothers us here in Jangali – aye, even while we're swilling back the black stuff for the sake of our souls, to keep us out of that Godmind's clutches after we're dead!" And he promises me that he'll hang on for our surprise. And he'll help if he humanly can – so long as it suits the junglejacks. "Can't commit us, sight unseen!"

'"Fair enough, Pet," I told him. "I'm sure you'll find it suits you. What's at stake is *big*."

'"And Yaleen isn't her own mistress?"

'"No more than I'm yours," said I.

'"Oho," says he, "we'll see about that!"

'So we did.'

All in all – a whiff of jealousy aside – I judged that Peli had done rather adroitly; and enjoyed herself into the bargain. Though Petrovy's comment didn't amount to an absolute promise, it was a whole lot better than a poke in the eye. The 'jacks had all flooded back to their patch of forest, but they were a proud mob. Once military – twice militant?

It was at Port Barbra that things really happened.

The Worm's priestess was highly popular in that town. Umpteen spectators turned out to see the *Crackerjill* tie up. Such was the throng that several women and girls got pushed into the water and almost came to grief squeezed between our boat and the jetty. They either swam clear or were fished out in time, unstung, and fortunately no men had ventured as close to the riverside as those who got a ducking.

As I've said before, Port Barbra is a tawdry, muddy slum of a place where the locals pay little heed to the graces of life such as clean streets or elegant housing. They wrap themselves up in hoods, scarves, veils, kerchiefs; as well as in their own inwardness.

On the afternoon of our arrival the people of 'Barbra were definitely more forthcoming. They didn't actually

85

cheer, but they did croon and sigh as if their voices were a wind in a great chimney.

Another sort of crowd also greeted us: a host of tiny midges. We on board were soon muffled up like the folk on shore, and were practising talking with our lips shut and squinting through half-closed eyelids.

'The worst it's ever been!' Peli groused.

'Mmm,' I agreed. 'Glad I'm titchy now. Less of me to bother.'

I observed that 'Barbrans didn't waste time and energy on slapping these pests or trying to waft them away from the areas of flesh left exposed. They just ignored this inconvenience – in the same style that they spurned the conveniences of life.

When the horde of welcomers at last dispersed, so too did the clouds of flies. Perhaps it was the people themselves who had attracted the pests, by congregating in such a mass. We weren't persecuted as badly again.

For me the next few days were busy, busy. A marquee had been erected near the quaymistress's shack – this was Port Barbra, remember, and the guild didn't wish to be ostentatiously at odds with local building codes. The entrance to the marquee was hung with curtains of muslin, to exclude unwelcome miniature visitors whom I, for one, had no wish to take to the *Ka*-store with us; should flies have *Ka*s and fall into the waiting jugs of current and be drunk, so that you had to share your afterlife with a zizzing midge. No, I'm joking. Fly-curtains were standard fittings on 'Barbra doors and windows to keep winged pests out of homes. This much comfort the locals allowed themselves, otherwise they would have gone mad; and such curtains increased their privacy. Alas, out of respect for a visiting priestess the local contractors rather outdid themselves on muslin drapes. As a result the tent grew stuffy and heada-chy. The year was dipping towards its finale by this time, thus the weather wasn't as hot as it might otherwise have been. Even so, we were deep in the tropics. I had to ask Lana to fan me with a huge leaf; which must have made me look positively pampered to 'Barbra eyes. Or perhaps this enhanced my image as exotic emissary of the Worm?

Anyway, I was busy; and Peli was busy too. She visited the local newssheet printer and enquired about Peera-pa, saying that she had an important message to deliver. The printer-*cum*-editor fellow was reticent (weren't they all, hereabouts?), but he assured Peli that he would ask around.

Peli brought back with her a copy of his weekly product, *Barbra's Bugle.* For the most part the contents seemed to consist of aimless gossip – aimless, because most of the names were concealed by initials, though maybe everyone in Port Barbra knew who was referred to. Actual news from the rest of the river was condensed into short snippets, run together and crammed into a box. What a contrast with the sophisticated repartee and tidbits of wisdom to be found in the flourishing Ajelobo rags only forty leagues downstream! Nor was the printing any too choice.

'He ought to have called it *Barbra's Bungle*,' joked Peli.

The headline story, about my own impending arrival at such and such a time aboard the *Crackerjill*, struck me as distinctly odd. It read less like news than like editorial, practically instructing readers to present themselves for a dose of the current (if they hadn't already enrolled via the quaymistress). Half way through, the column turned into a downright homily upon the *Ka*-store, which was described as '*the place where time stops and the plant of life becomes the death-seed, with all contained within alive for ever and ever*', or some such.

According to Stamno the 'Barbra newssheet was under

the wing of cult sympathizers. So maybe this *Bugle* was written partly in code? Maybe what I took for aimless gossip really consisted of secret messages and parables with quite other meanings, crystal clear to those who were in the know. Scanning the *Bugle* I began to get an even ickier feeling about Port Barbra than I'd had on previous visits; and about my book being printed here in the guise of a newssheet. The place was creepy. The lives of the locals were a strange charade.

Then two mornings later a little girl delivered a sealed envelope to Peli.

Inside was this message: *The one you are interested in will meet you and your little riversister outside the Bugle office when dusk is night. Both of you; but no one else.* The note was unsigned.

Peli got a chance to show me the note privately back on board just before lunch. It had been a hectic morning in the marquee and it looked like being an equally hectic afternoon. We might well have to extend our stay in Port Barbra from one to two weeks, thanks to popular demand; which was an improvement on extending our stay thanks to indifference, as at Guineamoy. Who would have thought so many people inhabited the environs – and were able to decode their local paper?

'"Little riversister" has to mean you, Yaleen.'

'No doubt.'

'So whoever sent this knows that you and me are as thick as thieves.'

'Right. So we're getting somewhere. How do I sneak ashore?'

'Eh? You can't possibly risk – '

'I can. I'm fed up with temples and tents and cabins and guards. Don't you worry about Donnah.'

'It's you I'm worried about, you chit.'

'Well, I'm *going*. The question is how. Could you carry me ashore wrapped in a rug?'

'Don't be daft. What would I be carting rugs ashore for? At dusk?'

'Okay, it'll be dusk. Still possible to see, but not too sharply. You disembark ordinarily, Peli. Pile some rubbish near the marquee – there's always plenty lying around there. Remember to take a bottle of oil with you. Soak the rubbish, stick a couple of tapers in and light 'em. Then you nip back along the quayside. Meanwhile I'll have crept along to the stern. *Whoosh* goes the bonfire. Immediate distraction! Guards and boatwomen rush to the bows. I'll jump. Just make sure you catch me.'

Peli groaned, but didn't argue further.

Suddenly she grabbed hold of me, and with an almighty heave tossed me several spans in the air.

'Hey!'

And caught me.

'Checking your weight,' she explained with a grin.

I suppose that also explained the groan. One of anticipation: weight-lifter style.

Dusk found me crouched behind a coil of rope astern, having second thoughts about this escapade. The drop from afterdeck rail to jetty looked a *long* way down.

But then flames flared beside the marquee. A voice cried, 'Fire!' Figures rushed towards the bows. And the figure of Peli loomed below. I scrambled. I threw myself.

'Oof.' Peli staggered back with me clutched tight, but she didn't fall over. Still clutching me, she trotted off through shadows, only setting me down – crushed breathless – when we gained the wooden walkway of Treegold Mall (which might better have been named Muck Street). Gazing back, we saw flames writhing high.

'Some bonfire,' I gasped.

'Um, maybe I piled stuff too close to the canvas. Good cover there, though.'

'Looks like you've torched the whole tent.'

The leaping flames soon died and the orange glow faded. Well, any idiot could quench a blaze with a whole river on tap. We went on our way through the darkling dirty thoroughfares.

The *Bugle* office on Bluecloud Boulevard was nothing grand. It was a low clapboard building with a few poky windows fronting the messy roadway. By the time we arrived there, stars were brightening in the gloom. I couldn't imagine that daylight would have improved the looks of the place, though Peli had described the office as running back a way, with good skylights.

I didn't get to enter. Waiting for us outside in deep shadow were two hooded and scarved shapes. One of them was burly, the other slight. The burly shape uncovered a lantern, producing a pool of light. The slight figure stepped forward.

'What was that fire?' The voice was hushed and soft, though far from diffident.

'Our little trick,' I said, 'to get away unnoticed. Are you Peera-pa?'

'Yes.' Peera-pa gestured at her henchmate. 'I believe you know my friend.'

The big person threw back her hood and loosened her scarf. Chopped-off pigtails, framing a large girlish face . . . it was Credence. The same Credence who had been boatswain of the *Spry Goose*! Who had tried to steal samples of the black current for the cult women. Who had marooned Marcialla up a tree, drugged and in danger of her life.

Credence who had deserted in Jangali, after I foiled her scheme.

None of which inspired much confidence, even granted that she'd been manipulated by the Worm.

'Hullo, little one,' said Credence. 'I forgive you, on account of all you have become.'

'That's nice of you. Forgive me for what?'

'For ruining my life as a riverwoman.'

'There might be two ways of looking at that! Marcialla's career wouldn't have been improved much by falling out of a tree and breaking her neck.'

'Ah, that was unfortunate. If only she'd seen sense.'

'Let's hope I don't have to be persuaded to see sense likewise.'

Peli drew me aside. 'Something wrong?' she murmured.

Peera-pa, used to conversing in murmurs, heard her clearly. 'Nothing is wrong. Just old history. Yaleen is safe with us.'

'She's safe with *me*, you mean,' asserted Peli. Peera-pa's eyes looked amused.

I said to Credence, 'I suppose you don't have as much trouble laying your hands on doses of black current these days?'

The former boatswain began wrapping up again. 'Hmm, it isn't as easy as all that. The guild make people drink it on the spot. They register names.' She didn't, mark you, say that it was impossible.

'Shall we go?' enquired Peera-pa.

'Go? Where? I thought we met here to discuss my book and Stamno's whereabouts.'

'We know where he is, Yaleen. He's with friends in Gangee. Your manuscript is safely in our hands. It will be printed.'

91

'Soon, I hope! You do realize that the Godmind is getting ready to zap everybody in the known universe?'

'For the sake of awful knowledge. Yes, so I understand. If that is what must be done to acquire such knowledge – '

'Then we're better off without it,' Peli said bluntly.

'I was going to say that, in that case, we are a mere span – to the Godmind's league. But still!'

'Still what?' growled Peli.

Peera-pa's voice was silky. 'Still, we have a priestess with us now. We can contact the black current directly. We can set foot upon the true path of time and being. In return, we shall publish a certain book right speedily.'

'So that's the deal?' I said. 'Stamno never mentioned any deal.'

Beyond the yellow pool of Credence's lantern it was black by now. Only a few distant windows down Bluecloud Boulevard showed smudges of illumination, while the stars above twinkled to themselves alone. I felt disadvantaged.

Peera-pa spoke gently. 'If anything effective can be done to save our cousins in the sky, you must know in your heart that the lever to achieve this cannot simply be some spontaneous outcry by your readers. Most people aren't interested in great truths.'

'They've been interested enough so far,' said Peli. 'In their tens of thousands! That's what Yaleen's first book achieved.'

'So her second book will have a similar effect? Pah! If you think that, you're a fool. People wish to save their *own* souls. Once that ambition is achieved, why strive further?'

'We've had some guarantees,' Peli said. 'Though I'm not naming names.'

Peera-pa chuckled. 'Political promises? Perhaps they'll be fulfilled – if it suits those involved. Really, what difference can that make? I'll speak more plainly. What possible difference – other than to salve your own conscience? Other than to exonerate Yaleen from any personal guilt in the cosmic massacre?'

Peli said, 'I don't see how she's to blame. Any more than me!'

'Quite. But anyone is to blame for something awful if they know about it and don't exert themselves to the utmost to stop it. Or if they adopt the wrong strategy – a strategy which *appears* to be bold, but which is really a lesser strategy – likewise they are blameworthy. So let's consider strategies, greater and lesser. To defeat the God-mind means to lock it up everywhere, not just to check it on one piddling little planet. The only way to do that is to discover the key which the Godmind searches for; *before* the Godmind finds it. You must search for the key to the Real – the truth-key. That's why you really sought me out; or else if not, it ought to be. If Yaleen hadn't sought me out, we should have sought her out soon.'

'You certainly fancy yourself!' said Peli. 'What do you know about any of this, compared with her?'

'We know how to look for the key, and where.' Peera-pa slid two fingers under her scarf and whistled into the night. Hand-lanterns appeared ahead of us, and behind. Hooded shapes approached. Peli flinched, but since there were at least half a dozen newcomers she subsided.

'We shall go into the hinterland,' Peera-pa told us. 'We will go to our private place.'

'What, by night?' I tried to keep a light tone to my voice. 'Isn't that carrying discretion a bit far?'

'We know our way, Yaleen. And at our private place there's a person you should meet. As to carrying, why, Credence will carry you. You can sleep in her arms. She's tireless.'

'What if I prefer being carried by Peli?' I said this, not

so as to burden Peli, but simply to check that Peera-pa's plans included her.

Apparently they did. 'Peli might stumble on a root. We don't want you hurt. Or tired out by a bumpy journey.'

'I guess riding Credence is a change from her telling me to swab the decks . . . Say, how long is this journey going to take?'

'We shall arrive by dawn.'

'And get back when?' demanded Peli. 'Donnah's guards are going to take this town apart.'

'With teeth and claws. What a delightful notion. Alas, they won't learn much. That's why we need to go inland – and quickly. Your silly bonfire may already have alerted them. Come!'

'There doesn't seem a lot of choice,' I said. There wasn't, either. And maybe, maybe, Peera-pa's plan was the right one.

Credence scooped me up in her arms. She arranged me so that my head rested on her shoulder.

At quite an early stage during our subsequent journey – down some winding track through pitch-dark forests – lulled by her surprisingly smooth motion, I nodded off.

What woke me hours later was the noise of Peli falling asleep. The ingredients were a thump, a crash, and loud confused moans.

A black army of tree-masts and a dark crowded canvas of foliage sailed overhead against a livid sky. Dawn was almost upon us. Where was I? What was going on? Moans were going on.

'Whatzzit?' I groaned, blinking and stiff. 'Peli!' I cried.

Black figures milled around the source of the noise – which became ripe, weary curses. A shape was hauled out of coaly shadows.

'S'nothing.' Credence yawned in my face. 'No crisis.'

'Peli!'

The shape blundered in our direction, shaking off the arms which tried to guide it, or restrain it.

'Where are you, Yaleen? You cried – ' Peli stopped short, just near me, and clutched at her nose. 'Oof!' It was too dark to see if she was bleeding.

'I'm here, Peli. I'm okay. What happened?'

Peera-pa's voice: 'She fell asleep on her feet, that's what.'

Peli mumbled, 'We must have tramped a hundred leagues this night.'

'Hardly!'

'I was dreaming. Then: *wham*.'

'She walked into a tree.'

'I feel half-dead.'

'That's a pessimist's view. Try to feel half-*alive*, instead. We'll arrive soon. Once we're there, we can all get some shut-eye.'

As full dawn crept closer, progressively more light soaked down through the trees. In consequence the contrast between brightening sky overhead and the dark forest of our journey diminished. Soon the sky was no longer obvious. The visible canopy of foliage now hid it.

The track which we were following led through a medley of coarsewoods interspersed with occasional ashen groves of ivorybone. The path hugged a meandering stream. In places where undergrowth was dense and scratchy, the path *was* the stream. We quit the guidance of this brook at a bend where a fallen jacktree sprawled rotting across the water.

Soon we came upon a huge boulder splotched with lichen. Behind, as if emerging from an invisible door in the rock, a pavement commenced: an actual pathway of flagstones. Our party fairly trotted along this pavement for a third of a league, winding between the trees. Then ahead the forest parted, opened up.

The pavement led into a long glade. Close at hand, a low stone bridge crossed the narrowest point of a marshy mere; above the sedges the air was fuzzy with gnats. Beyond stretched a great sward of voluptuous velvety moss, purple and violet as eggplant skin. That dark moss defied the light blue of the open sky above. It seemed to blot up the shafts of low sunshine lancing through the treetops – so that it still might have been night throughout the glade, except that you could see everything plain as day. Here was midnight magically made visible, as some nocturnal rodent might see it.

The sward rose up towards . . . a little palace! A palace which stood out against the moss like a precious Aladalia ornament upon a pad of velvet.

The palace had two storeys and looked to be octagonal. Hat-like, it wore a superimposed tile roof with eaves upswooping. Long leaden beaks jutted far out to spill rainwater clear of the curtain walls of gildenwood, polished and gleaming. Orange marble columns divided each wall from the next. Numerous tiny windows, set at random, were outlined by frames of bloodthread rubyvein. Each little window appeared to be of opaque wax-paper rather than glass.

What a splendid, enchanting, rich palace this was! That it should be found out here deep in the forests was an astonishment to me – though such an edifice, in tatty Port Barbra, might have been even more amazing.

'Our private place,' said Peera-pa.

Credence set me down at last.

I was too stunned to comment. Peli likewise. Or maybe she was still stunned from her encounter with that tree.

* * *

The stone pavement cut through the moss to the palace, which it encircled. As we were drawing close, I found my voice.

'But *why*? Why such a building?'

'All the usual reasons,' said Peera-pa. 'Keeps the rain out. Wildlife too.'

'No, but why so beautiful?'

'The path of truth is beautiful, Yaleen. If an answer isn't beautiful, how can it be right?'

'Oh. Is this the path of truth we're walking now?'

She chuckled. 'Commencing in the midst of nowhere; yet arriving at a marvellous destination? Perhaps!' She tossed back her hood. She lowered her black gauze scarf. For the first time I could scrutinize her features.

She was at once old, and young. By which I mean that her face was the face of a young woman, yet at the same time it was wizened. Her hazel eyes were lively, youthful – yet webbed around with wrinkles. Her hair was part auburn, part ashen grey. Her teeth were white and untarnished; the mouth which held them was puckered.

Here was somebody who had over-used the fungus drug. Were her limbs lithe and smooth, I wondered, or shrivelled?

Obviously she read my thoughts. She smiled enigmatically. 'It doesn't matter, this. You see, I have lived as long as anybody else has lived; namely, the whole of my life.' She slid a door aside on runners and called, 'We're here!'

The entry was hung about with muslin drapes, one behind another. A strong smell of herbs and spices drew my attention to little bags of popery dangling on strings; or is the word 'peppery'? Peera-pa held the first veil aside. Peli and I slipped through the various layers – she sneezing thunderously mid-way.

Within, the lower floor of the palace seemed to be all one

97

huge room; with eight, yes eight, sides to it. Various lacquered cabinets, red and black, hugged the walls. The floor mostly consisted of springy straw matting of the tight sort, pack-woven inside large cloth-edged frames which fitted neatly side by side. However, there were also several sunken pits containing piles of cushions, in all shades of red. In the pastel light diffusing through the paper windows, these pits looked like storm-tossed pools of blood. A broad brass stairway circled around upon itself, to gain the upper storey. Descending those stairs, carefully, came a bald fat man.

The man wasn't just fat. He was a pyramid of flesh. He wore a pink silk blouse of considerable volume, embroidered with flutterbyes, and matching trousers of even greater girth with a mauve sash tied around his equator. The blouse and trousers clung sweatily to breasts and paunch; though it was still early in the morning. When finally he achieved the floor, he waddled beaming towards us. His smile was a twisting mass of blubber.

'Peepy!' he panted.

'Papa,' said Peera-pa affectionately.

'Uh?' said I. 'Is this your dad?'

'No, Mardoluc is an honoured friend. And a wise one. That's why I call him Papa.'

The man squinted at me from amidst pouches of fat.

'Blessings, Yaleen!' he wheezed. 'I cannot easily kneel or bow. Blessings, none the less! Oh no I cannot easily bend myself to you. As soon fold a world in half.' A snorting noise commenced deep within him. This increased in volume as it penetrated through the layers to the outside. He wobbled violently as if massaged by hidden hands. Tears squeezed from his eyes. I decided that he was laughing.

Presently the convulsion subsided. Clutching his belly

with both hands – as if otherwise he might burst apart – the gross figure headed for the floor-pit closest by. He entered this like a boat launched down a slipway, displacing a wave; in this case, of cushions. Somehow he managed to rotate as he sank so that he came to rest upon his back, facing us.

He thumped cushions. 'Bless us, that you're here! Yaleen: come and talk to Papa Mardoluc!'

At this point Peli yawned; none too quietly. That yawn gave Peera-pa her excuse.

'Sleepy time,' she announced, 'for all but those who have slept already.' Linking with Peli, Peera-pa started to hustle her off in the direction of the stairway. Peli blundered along, confused. The rest of our troupe crowded in behind. So did I. Credence promptly picked me up and turned me around, while my legs were still busy walking. I felt like a wind-up toy automaton such as I'd seen kids playing with in Venezia. Pointing me back towards the pit, Credence gave me a push.

Unlike a toy, I turned again.

'No, no,' said Credence. 'You heard the lady. You've had your snooze. Stay and amuse Papa. Play with him. You might learn a few new tricks.'

'Hey! I'm not some fat ogre's plaything!'

Looming over me, she smiled nastily. 'He isn't going to *bother* you, dearie. What a grotesque notion. Whatever put such a fancy in your head?'

'You just did,' I muttered. Her smile became a smirk. 'Oh I get it!' I hissed. 'You've nobly forgiven me for ruining your life – but you don't mind a spot of venom on the side.'

'Dear me, and after I carried you all this way! I'm sure I don't know what you're on about, little priestess.'

'Don't you just.'

'Yaleen!' bleated recumbent Mardoluc.

'Is something amiss?' Peera-pa called from the stairway.

'No!' I bawled back. 'Everything's lovely!' So as not to afford Credence further cause for petty satisfaction, I headed for the fat man's pit under my own sails.

'Amiss!' cried Mardoluc. 'Amiss, is food. We'll need food, Peepy. Food for our guest, food for me. In proportion! The pot's on the hob upstairs.' He licked blubbery lips and flexed podgy fingers: a display which I decided wasn't aimed at me personally. Even so, I perched on the edge of the pit well out of reach.

So he'd been cooking; hence the sweat . . . As he wallowed expectantly, I found to my surprise that his gross conduct was actually whetting my appetite. There was a kind of, yes, blatant innocence about it, which I almost found endearing. Almost.

Cancel that 'almost'. Before long I found myself really regretting that I'd ever called him a fat ogre. (Put it down to nerves!) We got on like a house on fire.

The catalyst, the spark, was the meal.

Mardoluc wasn't any old cook. He was a master chef. What came down on trays to our pit was a dream: bowls of thick peppery bean and potato soup, vine leaves packed with minced lamb, broiled land-snails, sour curd with pollfish fritters (eccentric but yummy), sweetbread buns spread with lime jelly. Confronted with such foods one could only become the Complete Gourmand: both glutton and gourmet at once! Which Mardoluc certainly was, gluttony-wise; for this was just breakfast time. Yet he managed to combine the gutsiest exuberance with appreciative finesse in an infectiously persuasive blend.

He munched. He sucked his fingers. 'You need to slacken up, Yaleen. Relax.'

'Do I?' I nibbled and licked.

'Yes indeed. You're like a coiled spring. That's why you snap at people.' He seized a soup bowl. 'Glub-glub-glub-glub.' He actually said this as he drank; I kid you not. 'Slurp the stuff down, but savour it too.'

'Likewise, gobble your famous fungus?' I'd been picking at my food on the lookout for any fungi, whether whole or minced. Which was simply a waste of time. As I recalled, the cultists were supposed to use the fungus in powder form. The meal could have been laced with it, and me none the wiser. Maybe the fungus possessed a distinctive tang. Never having tasted any, how should I know?

'There you go again!' He emptied a last dollop of soup down his throat, and then his tongue was out questing into the bowl, lapping up the smears. 'That comes later, not now. So dig in; don't be shy. *That's* better!' He cheered me on as I began to do more justice to the stuffed vine leaves. He thrust a snail at me, expertly cracking the shell. 'Try one of these!'

Eventually I had to cry quits. There are limits.

By the time that stage arrived I felt sleek and sensual; and I'd joined Mardoluc lolling amidst the cushions. (Somehow, he'd managed to avoid spilling anything.) He had awoken a buried fire in me which so far had only peeked out in the form of flashes of jealousy at Mum and Peli; and he'd done so without anything overtly erotic occurring. (Else, I'm sure I would have screamed the palace down.)

How can I put it? Touch had transmuted into taste; and now I wanted to taste more experiences, and wilder, but in some different mode than usual. I'm aware that frustrated people often console themselves with food, but that wasn't the case here. Mardoluc was flesh supreme. Flesh-plus. Consequently he was more than flesh. His presence made me bigger and fleshier. He freed the woman hidden in the

101

child. He expanded me. This made me want to expand further still, into some new sphere.

'You are one fine cook,' I said.

He looked comically pained. 'Just *one*? Not two? Or three? Or a whole kitchen of cooks all rolled into one?' A tear rolled down his cheek (with difficulty).

'Sorry, chef!'

'Apology accepted! Ah me, but I'm still famished.'

'You can't be serious.'

'Oh I am. I'm starving. I have a hefty appetite for truth, too.'

So saying, we got down to business.

Truth. The truth about Mardoluc was that he had inherited a modest family fortune when he was barely out of his teens. The money came, of course, from trade in precious woods. Mardoluc's parents had been married ten years, with still no sign of an heir, when at his mother's persuasions they finally consulted a wise woman of the hinterland. She solved the problem – of sterility or impotence – with a potion. After Mardoluc's birth, however, his mother's womb had sickened, so that the boy would remain their only offspring ever; no daughter would inherit. When Mardoluc was ten, his mum had died. Heart trouble killed his dad a decade later.

Mardoluc only discovered the secret history of his conception upon opening his dad's death-letter. Presumably his dad spilled the beans in the hope of filling his heir with a new sense of responsibility. For had not Mum and Dad risked their health and mutual happiness to bring their son into the world? Whether accurately or no, his dad traced the genesis of his own heart condition back to that trip up-country and to the wise woman's medicine; not to mention the sickness of the womb which made his wife ail. Mardoluc, by his teens, had become something of a sensualist and epicure – hardly the sort of young fellow to hand over to with a light heart, unless he was first thoroughly dunked in cold water.

Mardoluc read the death-letter differently. To him it was clear that the wise woman in question had been a cultist; and that his mum and dad had conceived him by rutting whilst drugged. This accounted for the sensuality of his nature; and now his sensuality was pointed in a certain direction, namely the hinterland. Hitherto his epicurism had been cramped by the general squalor of Port Barbra; which was why he had lavished so much energy upon superb cuisine. Mardoluc was a creature of good taste, but only one sort of good taste – of the food variety – seemed possible in 'Barbra itself. Now he decided to search out his real home and extend the realm of his pleasures.

Yet the concept of a 'real home' begged a number of questions. Such questions as: 'Could I ever build a real home for myself anywhere in this world?' He knew that he might have fulfilled himself better in Ajelobo or far Aladalia. To be sure of this he would have had to sail to Ajelobo or Aladalia as a lonely passenger, unable to sail back again if he discovered he had made the wrong choice.

Questions such as this: 'My parents risked a lot to bring me into the world; okay, point taken. But where did they bring me *from*? What was I, before I was? Am I even the same person as I was yesterday?'

In Mardoluc's case good taste wasn't confined to the sensual domain but was a general cast of mind: composed of savour and discrimination. So whilst he fed his flesh excellently – increasing his already hefty anchor-hold on the world – he also asked himself some deep questions.

In the course of our tettytet he said, 'How much do

you remember of your own first origin, Yaleen?' And he answered himself, thus: 'Why, nothing! At first your mind wasn't capable of knowing that it existed. It had to learn existence little by little. When it had learnt, and when you'd become a person with an identity, everything which went before became hidden in a timeless mist. You had congealed out of that mist, like a roux stiffening a milky sauce, but never at any single definable moment.

'Perhaps something akin happens throughout life. Identity isn't born of communion with the past. It's caused by *loss* of the past. Forgetfulness forges the person; not memory.'

'Till we enter the *Ka*-store, Papa!' I'd taken to calling him that. 'When we die, our whole life is ever-present to us.'

'Ah yes. We're only fully present after we die. Not before. Do you know, I suspect that we might have been looking at existence the wrong way round? Could it be that our *Ka*s originate not at birth, but at death? Could it be that they give us our being in retrospect? Could it be that from out of the illuminated *Ka*-state after death we project a cone of awareness backwards through our whole lives like the beam of a lanthorn – a beam which fades out, the further that it pierces into the past? You have twisted back into the past, Yaleen. Thus it is written in *The Book of the Stars*. What say you?'

'Gosh, I dunno. So you've read Stamno's copy?'

'But of course. The copy's back in 'Barbra now.' He waved a hand dismissively. 'What say you?'

'One thing I do know: the *Ka*-store can't last forever. If our sun ever blazes up and burns the world, or if its fires die and our world freezes, I guess the Worm will die too. Where *Ka*s go to *afterwards*, seems a good question.'

'Maybe they don't go, but come. If only we could solve

this teaser! The moment flees; we cannot stop it – only slow it with a drug. You twisted back into the past, Yaleen. If only you could halt the flow of time – without having to die! We might learn what time is, and existence too. Then we could really fight the Godmind.'

'So that's what you want from me. Do you know what the Worm wants, Papa? It wants me to contact worms on other worlds. It thinks I ought to jump out of a balloon and kill myself.'

'A balloon? I don't follow.'

'I should go up in a hot-air balloon and leap out of the sky. Splat. Then it can scoop me up and send me through *Ka*-space on my travels.'

'My proposal seems rather less drastic, don't you think?'

'I wonder. I do wonder.'

'Are you worrying that you might end up like Peepy, prematurely aged? Or like me, a monstrous mountain of lard, a tun of tummy? Oh I fully admit that this fullness of fat can't all come from eating!' He grinned. 'How could mere eating have done this to me?'

'A complete mystery,' I said.

'I'm thirty-two years old. Soon I'll have a heart attack, just like my own dear Papa. The circle of my existence will be complete. Pretty big circle, though, stretching all the way around me! Big enough, maybe, to bend time itself? If you could but show me how . . . Time might stop and I might live forever inside a single moment. Ah dreams, ah just desserts, ah extraordinary dinners!' I couldn't tell how much was joke and how much in deadly earnest; but if plea this was, he didn't stoop to beg or wheedle.

'One use of the drug won't warp you,' he promised.

Well, one use of it hadn't warped Marcialla; just screwed her up for a while.

'Maybe,' I said, 'you can't actually stop time entirely. If

you get close to doing so, maybe time shifts you – to some
other time?'

'Ah! Now, why's that?'

'Perhaps if time did stop completely, everything would
have to stop existing?'

'We would only find non-existence: is that what you're
saying?'

I shook my head. That didn't seem right. I'd spent time
– no, not time exactly; I'd spent a period of 'never-ever' –
in the void. In the void there was nothing. But the void
itself wasn't nothing. The void was bubbling and simmering
with –

'Not non-existence,' I said. 'Pre-existence is what you'd
find. The potential to exist.'

As we talked, it became increasingly obvious to me that
probably that very same day I was going to sample some
fungus powder, no doubt in a black current cocktail. Papa
Mardoluc had gained some curious insights by use of the
drug; and the same drug had acted as a *catalyst* upon the
Worm too. (New words: use 'em, or lose 'em!)

Later, half a dozen more women arrived accompanied by a
couple of men. They bore baskets of provisions. Mardoluc
explained how a thriving little farm had been set up nearby
especially to supply the palace. This farm even had its own
miniature river, according to him. A stream had been
deepened, widened and diverted round in an ox-bow shape
for part of its length. A bucket-chain, worked by a windmill, quickened the flow by transferring water from the tip
of the downstream 'horn' across to the upstream horn;
hence the presence of pollfish on the breakfast menu.

Presently Mardoluc heaved his way upstairs to see to
lunch. Since he declined my offer of culinary assistance, I
was left to my own devices and I went outside on to the

moss-sward so as to be alone of my own free choice rather than by default.

In full daylight the moss appeared darker than ever. The living velvet had become a black mirror, a lustrous hummocky expanse of polished jet. It reminded me of a certain lava-field near Firelight. Here, however, the surface might *look* as hard as could be – stiff, slippery – yet really it was soft and yielding. My eyes told me lies about it. Only touch told the truth. Earlier on I'd been leery of touch. Now I sank my fingers into springy vegetable flesh.

Flies seemed to shun the moss. Maybe they could smell something which I couldn't smell. More likely the darkness of the sward confused their simple senses. The sward confused me too, but I adored it.

No, that was *why* I liked it! It upset my balance – in a way which made me feel more agile within myself.

Meanwhile, what of the *Crackerjill*? My absence would be a certainty by now. Peli's, too. The possible consequences bothered me a bit. The river guild could hardly cut off one of my feet in reprisal, the way they had cut off Tam's hand. Even so, they might send Peli away from me as punishment. They might beach her in 'Barbra as tit for tat for her part in my misdemeanour. I would have ruined her life; and I could hardly see Peli becoming a bosom-buddy of Credence's.

While I was brooding about this, and trying to imagine agile solutions, sprightly outcomes, Peli herself emerged from the doorway. She looked more edgy than refreshed.

I scrambled up and was just starting to reassure her that we were in safe hands – when Peera-pa followed her through the veils, wrinkling her nose.

'You can relax,' I was saying.

'Shut up, will you?' muttered Peli. 'I just farted in there,

107

that's what. I didn't think anyone would notice. But it smelt like a kitchen-full of fried poppadums.'

'Oh dear.'

'I was amazed.'

'That's quite a nice smell, poppadums.'

'Not when it comes out of someone's arse.' Peli shifted away, stared at the sky, whistled innocently.

'Ahem,' said Peera-pa.

'Oh hullo,' said Peli. I giggled helplessly.

Peli made a bluff lunge at conversation. 'Er, why does that fat fellow call you Peepy, then?' she asked.

Peera-pa pulled up her hood and half-veiled her face.

'Perhaps because I only peep at the Truth instead of peering steadily.' She sounded hurt. 'A glimpse is better than being blind!' Aye, and perhaps her name hinted how strangers *peeped* at Peera-pa's young-and-ancient face?

'Dum-di-dum-di-dum,' hummed Peli.

A whole kitchen-full of big thin crinkly flour-biscuits, sweaty with boiling oil! *Papa*-dums! I sniggered and hastily slapped myself across the cheek.

'Sorry,' I said.

'For what?' asked Peera-pa, staying veiled.

'Thought a fly bit me. Forget it, forget it. It's nothing.'

Perhaps Peera-pa had come out with the intention of confiding in me, as Papa Mardoluc had done. (Unless she had simply popped out for some fresh air!) Alas, if so, Peli's fart and its aftermath had blown that tender chance away.

'Hmm,' said Peera-pa. 'We should have lunch now. Empty bellies, empty brains; empty bowels and gasbags!'

'I'm still stuffed tight from breakfast,' I said. 'Papa's such a *splendid* cook.' Might honest flattery retrieve the situation?

'You'll be starving later on. It's better to fill up beforehand.'

'Before I take the timestop drug?'

She nodded, as though this was taken for granted. Perhaps Papa had already tipped her the wink, that I would.

'Incidentally, Yaleen, I ought to advise you that some participants may be more interested in the erotic aspects.'

'We're not prudish. Are we, Peli?'

'Dum-di-dum. Oh no.'

'That's their chosen path. You two won't be involved.' Peera-pa turned back to the doorway. Over her shoulder she added, 'Peli can be, if she wishes. Assuming that she hasn't put everyone off.' She disappeared through the veils.

'Oh sod,' mourned Peli. '*How* can I go back inside?'

'Um, sweet as roses?'

'Sweet as what?'

'Roses. The Godmind's favourite flowers. Never exported to the colonies.'

'Oh, those.'

And so to lunch: of snakemeat in aspic, galantines, salads, quiches, stuffed bluepears. I don't know how Mardoluc managed, either in the preparation or in the consumption. Trays sat everywhere and people moved from one to another, continually changing places – except for Papa in his pit, to whom mighty tidbits were brought whenever anyone shifted. The meal was like a weird change-your-partners dance, or a kids' game of musical cushions. I didn't notice anyone conspicuously avoiding Peli; though with everyone, us included, bobbing up and sitting down elsewhere, you never knew where you were.

I did notice Credence staring fixedly at me, at one point, like a cat intent on a flutterbye. She hastily adopted a sweet smile. Peera-pa, unveiled once more, dipped into our orbit amiably enough then out again. I exchanged pleasantries with many of the cultists, and they with me. In the midst of all, conducting the food-dance, reposed Mardoluc.

Finally, Peera-pa clapped her hands. The trays were all whisked back upstairs – whither Peli and I and others all repaired briefly to visit the privies.

Once we had all reassembled in the big room, Peera-pa unlocked one of the lacquered cabinets. Within, were bottles of an oily yellow liquid with several fingers of sediment in the bottoms; numerous glasses; and a few phials full of darkness which I had no difficulty in identifying as the substance of the Worm.

Peera-pa unstoppered the phials, emptied these into one of the yellow bottles and shook vigorously so that sediment and oil and blackness were mixed into a turbid cocktail. She agitated a couple of other yellow bottles too, without adding anything.

'Today,' she said to the assembly, 'Papa and I will pierce the veil of fleeting phenomena in company with the priestess of the current, blessed be she. We three shall follow the black way. Monitors will be Credence and Zelya and Shooshi. Everyone else will follow the usual amber path.'

'Excuse me, but what are these paths?' I asked.

Peera-pa indicated the different bottles.

'Oh. And what are monitors?'

'Monitors don't take any drug. They stay in ordinary time, to watch over you. When you speed up afterwards, they ensure that no harm comes.'

'And they see to our nourishment!' Mardoluc had hauled himself out of his pit by now and joined the rest of us. 'The drug takes about ten minutes to act,' he told me. 'The slowing effect can last for a good five hours, though it's strongest earlier on. Then the speed-up takes over – '

110

'And we gobble all the left-overs. I've seen the drug in action.'

'Left-overs! Tut, you insult me. There's a whole new feast awaiting.'

'Those who wish to take partners may now disrobe,' announced Peera-pa.

Both men from the farm and four women undressed. They jogged up and down for a while, showing off.

Peera-pa distributed glasses of the amber liquid first of all; and Peli wound up with one in her hand.

'Wait a mo,' she said. 'Why shouldn't I be a monitor?'

Credence answered, 'You've no experience. Drink up, now!'

'I ought to keep an eye on Yaleen.'

'You'd find it very boring.'

'What, me, as can keep watch for hours without fidgeting?'

A chuckle rumbled from deep within Mardoluc. 'In that case you're an ideal subject for the drug.' Other people were already downing their amber drinks.

Credence gave a negligent shrug. 'It's up to you. We can hardly pour the stuff down your neck. But you might easily misinterpret what you see, seeing as you know fart all about it.'

Peli flushed redder than usual.

'*Which* might make you interfere inappropriately,' agreed Mardoluc. 'You might do something we'd all regret.'

'It's okay, Peli,' I murmured. 'Honest, Papa knows best.'

'*Fart* all,' repeated Credence. 'Be a good big sister, hmm? Show an example.'

'Damn it,' swore Peli and swallowed her drink.

Credence patted her on the arm. 'Take my advice; pick a quiet spot, sit down and calm down. Here, I'll find you one – where you can watch the love-making, if you like. That's always nice to meditate on.'

Indeed, those who had taken their clothes off were already occupying one of the pits and engaging in gentle preliminaries.

'It's all a question of timing,' I heard Credence remark, as she drew Peli away.

Of the cultists who were still clad, one woman had lain supine on the matting. Another was kneeling. A third sat hunched over her knees. Several still stood, and looked like staying that way. It was then that I cottoned on to the reason why the numerous windows were tiny and opaque. This must be to stop participants from being blinded should the sun stare in their eyes while they were slowed, and no monitor happen to notice.

Peera-pa handed Papa and me our dark drinks. She raised her own.

'We three will hold hands. That way, I hope we may commune. It's quite possible in timestop. You being priestess makes this highly probable.'

'Does it? I shan't have much of a view round Papa's belly.'

'The view you seek is within,' she said.

'Okay. Cheers.' I drank. So did they. Shooshi relieved us of our glasses. Peera-pa, Papa and I linked hands.

The first thing I noticed about being drugged was that I'd been like this for an immensely long time. Yet the experience had only just begun; I was aware of that too. There was simply no borderline to mark the change. Once crossed – as soon as I realized the alteration – the borderline itself receded infinitely; vanished. The immediate past fled away. My memories were of a timelessness to come.

I knew now where Papa had got his idea about how we

112

emerge as full persons from out of a fog which, thereafter, hides the nature of what we were *before-we-were*. My own sensations were similar. I had gained Time – some sort of absolute time – by losing touch with ordinary time. Here was the same kind of 'never-ever' as I'd experienced in *Ka*-space during my crazy homeward flight from Earth.

Indeed, for a moment (but a moment of what magnitude?) *then* and *now* connected up seamlessly. Past event and present event were one. Whatever had occurred during ordinary time between whiles became an ox-bow lake of happenings – something pinched off from the stream of never-ever.

For a moment (but a moment of what order?) I thought I understood the means by which I had twisted back through time. I hadn't slid down a ladder of years, which everyone else must needs climb upward. I had simply floated from the outflow of the oxbow of events, back into the inflow; for both lay side by side in the never-ever.

When that had happened, I'd been dead; detached from the world. Now, however, the world confronted me – in the shape of Mardoluc's belly mainly, but also including his podgy hand holding Peera-pa's (I could see that), a patch of golden wall, a distant wax-paper window outlined in bloodwood.

As I stared fixedly, belly and wall and window began to blank out.

After an immeasurable while, the world came back, glowing with the message of its existence!

I had *blinked*; that's what. I had blinked my eyes. The blink had lasted for dark ages.

It came to me now that the whole world was actually winking in and out of existence constantly; yet we never noticed, because of the pace of time. Yes, the world forever came and went, just as it had done in that eyeblink!

113

For an age the world glowed and vanished and glowed again. Why should it remain the same, each time it returned? Why should it not be different?

Presently the answer became clear: the world remained constant because it was only a shadow. It was the shadow of the void. The shadow of nothing is something. The shadow of blackness is light. The shadow of a *Ka* is a person. The shadow of Potential is objects, things, events.

You can't change shadows by grasping them. You have to grasp the original. But how can you grasp a void?

I'd gone back through time, but I hadn't changed anything. I'd been scared to try – in case I vanished. Everything had to happen exactly as before.

I was breathing ever so slowly, in and out. His hand and hers grasped mine. Increasingly I became aware of the pressure of palms and fingers. My nerves had taken so long to pass the message on that when it finally arrived, it wasn't a whisper but a shout. Hearing this message of touch coming in so slowly, my brain opened its ears wide to hear it. Was it thus with those lovers rubbing against each other in the pit? Every feathery touch became a huge caressing wave? And orgasm itself, a volcano?

Aha, little priestess! Ho there, Peepy, we've done it! This way. Over here! Join in, do!

Not only possible, I told you, but probable! Rejoice!

Whilst simultaneously . . .

Yaleen!

Worm?

It's me, all right. But you're so quick.

Quick?

Compared with sluggish old me. You're time-slowed, aren't you? I've done that too. Part of me can match you for a while; the rest can catch up later. How's tricks? Given any more thought to my proposal?

114

About jumping out of a balloon?

Either that, or some other method. 'Tisn't as though you lack the knack of dying.

I wasn't planning on becoming an expert.

I'm one, and it hasn't done me any harm.

Come off it, Worm. You've never died.

Ah, but thousands have died into me. I know ten thousand deaths, and more. Things are getting critical, Yaleen. Your first incarnation has been dead about a year and a quarter. She'll be blowing up the Moon in a few more weeks.

Quite a few. Two score or so.

Time flies.

Not at the moment!

Why are you hanging back? What is it that scares you?

Being killed, old pal. Being tossed willy-nilly halfway to nowhere. You lost me last time, in case you've forgotten.

I have a stronger grasp now. I've analysed your last flight, in as much depth as I'm able, and I do believe I've figured out how to steer you to a worm-world.

Ho hum.

Worm of the River: is that you? This was Peera-pa, sounding somewhat awed.

Mardoluc was less abashed. *Excuse me: is this a private quarrel, or can anyone join in?*

We aren't quarrelling, said the Worm, *we're merely discussing tactics.*

Can you slow time at will? asked Peera-pa. *And can you dream the True which lies behind phenomena?*

Can you stop time completely? Mardoluc asked.

Me? Er . . . not quite yet. Look, folks, I really can't hang around much longer. I'm losing touch with myself. I'll see you all when you die. Bye!

Hang on! I cried. But the Worm departed, with what seemed to me like suspicious haste.

Mardoluc sighed. *Oh dear. So near, yet so far. Shall we show Yaleen the five rites of contemplation?*

Yes, that might bring a breakthrough.

What are those? I asked.

Techniques of ours, he said. *There's the rite of duration and the periodic rite. Then there's the ephemeral rite and the instantaneous rite and the synchronous rite, which is what the time-slowed lovers are busy at . . .*

What kind of breakthrough?

Why, to being! exclaimed Peera-pa.

Oh, you mean to those shapes that cast the shadows?

You can actually see those? Peera-pa sounded a bit awed once again.

She already glimpsed them in Ka-space, Peepy. She says so in her book. Remember the riddle of the raven and the writing desk? Remember how she guessed that the void dreams the shape of our universe, unawares? She already knows more than the River-Worm knows. But she doesn't know what she knows.

I'll say I don't, I said.

That's because you haven't disciplined yourself, Yaleen. You've gobbled knowledge like a cat let loose on a finger-kissingly cooked bouillabaisse of butterfish. The cat doesn't know the soup; it just feeds. In its haste, it doesn't really taste. Next moment it will catch and scrunch a fly.

How do you know a cat doesn't appreciate good cooking? Maybe a crunchfly for afters tastes as good as a crouton? (I didn't really believe it!)

There you go, off at a tangent.

Huh. You mentioned cats. I was talking about shapes that cast shadows – which I happened to glimpse just a bit ago, before you two joined me!

Really? There's hope for you yet! Let's instruct you in the first rite, of duration.

Okay, if it'll pass the time.

116

No, you mustn't pass time. Time must pass you. Start by observing what you see. Next, try to observe what you can't *see. Look in the gaps! Catch the breath of Being on the hop, between in and out. Usually the world is breathed too fast for us to notice . . .*

Immeasurable intervals passed by.

I didn't become too adept at this breath-of-Being business. Nor did my two instructors seem unduly adept; though I guess they had to be a long way ahead of anyone else I'd ever met. Maybe the Cognizers of Ambroz's world could have given Papa and Peepy a tip or two, but again maybe not.

Anyway, whilst I was busy observing and not-observing, something sinister started to happen. Credence loomed slowly into view, close by Papa. With what seemed immense patience she began prising Peepy's hand out of Papa's grasp – and suddenly I lost touch with the two of them!

At a snail's pace Credence slid her leg in front of Papa, as a pivot. Sluggishly she heaved.

I had all the time in the world to work out her intention. I even managed to loosen my own hand slightly from Peepy's. I even succeeded in shifting ever so slightly aside.

By now the something-sinister had become something very nasty indeed. How I tried to escape! And how useless it was to try!

Slowly Papa toppled. His bulk bore down on me, while Credence slid from sight. His huge belly began to push me over backwards. Slowly I fell – and the mountain of Mardoluc followed me down.

Oh yes, I had plenty of time to observe what was going on. And what was going on was a 'tragic accident', during which poor little Yaleen would be crushed to death by the

117

enormous chef who had alas lost his balance. Crushed, suffocated – one, or both.

Where the shit were Shooshi and Zelya?

Upstairs, no doubt! Sent up there on some pretext by Credence, who would now doubtless be up there too. She would distract and delay the two monitors – establishing her alibi in the process – then after a suitable interval she would pop back to the head of the stairs, spy the horrid mishap, and shriek.

Under normal conditions I don't suppose that Credence could possibly have thrown Mardoluc. He had to be time-slowed, unable to readjust his balance. So who would credit that she *had* thrown him? Not Papa or Peepy, I feared. Credence had stationed herself quite astutely before interfering.

I hit the matting, slowly-o. And he crushed down on me, oh so slowly-o.

Damn the Credence bitch!

No, wait. When Credence had acted treacherously before – that time when she suspended the drugged Marcialla high up a jungle-giant – it had really been the Worm who was responsible! My old pal had admitted as much. The Worm had played on Credence's dreams; had steered and manoeuvred her without her knowing it.

The Worm had just bragged that it *knew ten thousand deaths*. Ten thousand ways of dying. And it wanted me dead. In Credence's mind it could soon find anti-Yaleen grievances to bring to the boil. It had taken a quick look at the set-up here, and broken contact with indecent haste . . .

Mardoluc's mass pressed down fiercely.

The mat beneath and the belly above soon lost any bounce or sponginess. They were twin slabs of granite, squashing together – with me sandwiched in the middle. I was buried alive, and a mountain was being piled on me pound by pound, tun by tun.

Oh yes, the Worm had manipulated Credence. I was sure of it. Credence was just a dupe. And Mardoluc? Oh he was the fall-guy, for sure.

The Worm might know ten thousand deaths, but I bet it never knew a death such as this one.

Being shot by Edrick had been quick. Shrivelling, freezing and bursting in the wreck of the rose garden on the Moon had taken a while longer; it hadn't been interminable. This was.

Now my ribs were giving way. Slowly, but slowly.

I was nailed to the bottom of a lake, with half a league of water overhead, trying to drag a bucket of air down from the sky for my lungs; in vain. I was impaled by slow rods of blazing pain. I was torn apart inside. I was squashed as flat as a fleuradieu under a pile of books. Ever so slowly.

How I begged to die. Permission denied. Denied. I could repeat it for a hundred pages. For this went on. And on. And on.

After the hundredth, or thousandth, stage of my death: that was when my mind snapped and I went mad.

PART THREE
All the Tapestries of Time

It's a weird old business, going mad. Going mad isn't something which just happens to you. It isn't like getting trapped in a thunderstorm, or catching a chill. It's something which you *help to happen*.

You know that you're beginning to go mad. So you experiment with the madness. You give it a nudge here and a shove there. That's because you have to escape. When you're trapped in a vice that's squeezing you intolerably, and when this just goes on and on; when you can't die, or even faint – madness is the only way out, make no mistake.

Your mind-paths start to go astray. They bend. They deform. So you help them bend more. Your mental links start to snap, to dangle down into depths where you can hide. You follow them down gladly.

Your self splits up. You become separate selves, part-selves. Nobody knows these new persons, thus nobody can capture them and hurt them; not easily! Not even *you* knew they were inside you. No more than you paid attention to the workings of your womb and spleen and heart.

Imagine a body splitting up into independent heart, and spleen, and womb. Imagine each organ going its own way, toddling off on tiny legs. Now the organs of your mind do likewise.

The funny thing is that each mind-organ on its own seems more complete – more fully furnished, competent, consistent – than *you* ever did before, with all your ragged edges and loose ends!

These mind-organs, these part-selves are as the different cabins in an enormous boat.

This is the biggest boat you have ever sailed in. It isn't a mere *boat*. It's a legendary galleon – and argosy, and more! A river is too small to float it. It needs a whole sea.

You've grown not lesser by splitting, but larger.

A few cabins are bare and austere; a single oil lamp lights those. But for the most part, oh the furnishings! The panels of gildenwood and rubyvein, the ivorybone shelving, the chairs of hoganny, the ebon scritoires inlaid with pearly shell, the voluptuous bedding, the handbasins of mottled marble, the silver sconces, the bluecrystal candeliers and chandelabra ablaze with candles which never burn low or drip wax . . !

Most of all, the tapestries.

A tapestry adorns one wall of each cabin. Portholes are clamped tight, wearing thick brass lids; it is the tapestry which weaves the view instead.

So here's a view of dusty Pecawar when you were a little girl (before you became a little girl again). Here, of broad Aladalia when you dallied innocently with Tam. There, of the spinach purée jungles by Tambimatu . . .

Of the storm-lashed Zattere in Venezia.

Of the star-dunes of the eastern desert when you were dead, a stowaway in Lalia's memories . . .

Those cabins which are bare of luxury are set so deep beneath the waterline that if you did undog their brass port-covers the water outside would be as black and solid as a coal seam. Even though you don't go near the portholes you're aware of this.

Why should you go near them? Those shuttered portholes are your protection. As are the cabin doors, which all stay locked.

To move from one cabin to another you don't use doors and dart along corridors and up and down companion ways. Oh no.

Bend of hull, contour of deck and bulkhead, make the space of each cabin unique to itself. And each cabin is a separate person, a part of yourself. In order to reach another cabin you need only *fit yourself* to the right shape. That's the knack. You shift there immediately.

That's why the invading pirate enemy can't catch you. As soon as pain lays its hand on a doorknob you're off somewhere else.

But beware: if your madness isn't clever enough you might lose the knack. You might end up fastened away for your own safety in the most sunken cabin of all, so deep that no enemy could reach it by diving, so well concealed in the keel that your foe could spend the whole voyage forcing entry on the upper decks without ever scenting you. Your madness might swallow you – and then it might *swallow itself*.

So therefore: flow with the madness. Keep shifting. Dart from cabin to cabin, and from self to self.

Your madness is many things.

And you are many.

Where does this fine argosy sail to? Where's its destination? Why, anywhere in any tapestry! Your madness steers the vessel by shifting you from side to side like cargo.

In the eyes of the foe your galleon may seem like a bumboat or a wherry, something paltry. Your foe only glimpses a bit at a time. You alone know your vessel's true many-chambered immensity.

Shifting, shifting, you die. You can't avoid dying. And your galleon becomes a *ship of* Ka-*space* . . .

Spinning-top in a blue void. Bodiless in empty sky-space. Nothing visible but azure light . . .

Nothing at all?

Faintly you still sense cabins and tapestries.

Concentrate!

One tapestry takes on hue and texture. The rooftops of up-and-down Verrino. Plus river. Here's a tapestry such as poor dead Capsi might have woven high atop the Spire, had he crafted panoramas with needle and silk instead of pen and ink.

Sunshine shimmers on wet roofs; rain must have showered recently. Sunlight also sparkles on the river, showing how it flows. Clouds shadow-dapple the riverscape and shore. Their shadows slowly drift across the fabric like grey bruises.

An inky ribbon swims into sight from the south. It speeds along the midstream. Suddenly it ripples free of the river. Rising, it flaps bannerlike upward towards you.

The Worm's ugly head dwarfs buildings. Its body eclipses the whole river. But it doesn't dwarf you. Framed within the tapestry, the Worm is a huge *miniature*.

The head wavers. It quests about. You know you can't play hide-and-seek with the Worm the way you could to escape the torture-foe. But maybe you can fool it.

The Worm's head pops right out of the tapestry.

Gotcha! My, that was quick work, getting yourself killed so soon. Glad you saw sense. Well done, Yaleen.

Did you say quick? I was pressed to death for a year and a day!

Nonsense! You and I were chatting, oh, not an hour ago. So what happened?

You know very well.

Don't!

126

So take a look. Who's the master of ten thousand deaths? You are! Try another one on for size.

Um, I'm trying . . . Can't quite seem to find . . . Odd! Something's clouding it. In fact, you seem a bit odd yourself – as though you aren't all there.

(Do you hear a footfall in one of the dark corridors of your galleon?)

Damn it, Worm! Credence tripped Mardoluc. She threw the fat bugger. And he squashed me to death ever so slowly.

I'm really cut up to hear that.

Hypocrite, you arranged it! You used Credence the way you used her against Marcialla that other time. That's why you scrammed in such haste – to get busy burrowing in her brain, urging and prompting.

Gosh, Yaleen, but you're my friend.

So you'd do anything to ensure the pleasure of my company, including crushing me to death?

Gosh, I'm sorry. If only you'd taken my advice.

Hmph!

Please don't be bitter.

Bitter? Why should I be bitter? Off on my travels, aren't I? So let the shapes of power dance! Let's see how I'm going to find the worms of other worlds. Oh, do get on with it!

You're in such a rush, all of a sudden. Something's wrong.

(Hidden cabins, hidden tapestries, hidey holes, alternatives . . . and footsteps, creeping too close for comfort.)

Maybe that's because I'm the wrong shape. Such as: flat as a pancake? And who was whining about time, not so long ago? Just a few weeks left till the end of the world, nag, nag!

(The footsteps pause.) *That's possible, Yaleen.*

I'll say! The Godmind'll be mindburning everyone before you can sing out 'Jawgee Pawgee made 'em cry'. Oh, it'll clap the telescope of time to its eye. It'll spy out the key to existence in a trice. And zap you with it. So let's get busy, hey?

127

(Sound of footsteps retreating in panic.)

Very well. Pay attention. Last time, you followed the psylink back to Eeden and became a cherub. This time I'll give you an extra shove. What's more, I'll armour your Ka against being reborn. Assuming that I've got it right you'll swing around Earth and fly off along another psylink. You'll follow a psylink that's ravelled or tainted to a world where there's a worm in residence . . .

(Shapes of power begin feeding you your sailing orders, setting the canvas of your *Ka*-ship. The tapestry has vanished.)

. . . You won't be reborn. You'll simply share people's heads, the way you did with that heartwood porter and that eelwife.

How do you know about them?

I've been reading your record while we talked. Mind you, your record's strangely patchy. Can't figure out why . . .

(Faint tread of an intruder once again?)

Don't bother! What happens then?

I'll be keeping a tighter rein on you. Once you've contacted another worm and wised it up to the situation I'll yank you straight back here – thus providing a direct link with my new ally – then I'll pump you outward again to hook another worm.

(The shapes of power continue priming you whether you pay attention or not.)

It'll just be two or three worlds – against hundreds!

What's up with you? One moment you're keen as mustard. The next, you're pussyfooting.

What's wrong is that I haven't any choice *in the matter!*

(And you need choice. Lots of choice. Many cabins, many tapestries, many alternatives! Last time when you were in *Ka*-space on your way back home you saw how choices could be made. How a raven could be a writing desk. Yet you chose to be a baby girl in Pecawar, marking

128

time and repeating yourself. Ah, but *then* you weren't mad
– and many!)

All in a good cause, Yaleen!

If you say so.

That's my girl!

(The shapes of power fade . . .)

*Hang on! What about afterwards? When the great victory is
won; when I'm back here for good?*

*Afterwards, welcome to the Ka-store. Where you can relive
any life you choose.*

Relive – aye, and not change a single detail.

*You'd rather be alive again? Hmm. Do you suppose your
mother might be carrying Petrovy's child?*

No thanks! I've no wish to be anyone's little baby again.

You are hard to please.

*What about all the loose ends I've left behind? What about
Tam, stranded in Pecawar? What about the loose end of his
arm? What about you – stopped short at Aladalia? What
about men never being able to sail again? What about – ?*

You can't be responsible for everything.

(Why not, if there are enough of you?)

*That's Godmind megalomania, Yaleen. Are you sure you're
quite in your right mind?*

(Footfall on a companion way . . .

(Right mind, port mind; south mind, north mind. Aft
mind, for'ard mind, 'tween-decks mind.)

*I feel super. Never better. I'll settle for the Ka-store. Let's
get on with the job.*

Right!

This time, no gentle pat on the back sends you zipping
through *Ka*-space. You're picked up and hurled through
the storm-front, through the blue void. Surely the Worm
must have noticed that it was heaving not a cockle-shell
but an argosy? No. The weight of a *Ka* stays the same:

zero. Onward your *Ka*-ship sails, through a nothingness simmering with potential . . .

If you were many, would you see better? That's what you wondered once before.

That's the Godmind's project: to set fire to minds on a hundred worlds, to make a many-fold *Ka*-lens – and in that moment to try to master time, and Being.

The void bubbles. The void breathes.

You once felt that you were on the brink of a transformation. Then the Worm yanked you home. You chickened out.

The void dreams the universe. But the void is unconscious. The universe has consciousness, but it can't control the breath of Being. A strong force, the inertia of normality, rules the universe. So the universe always chooses the same state as before. It sustains itself; limits itself.

In *Ka*-space, the weak force rules. The force of choice. Yet no one chooses.

It's said in old myths that wizards could change men into toads, stones into bread. Those wizards must have tapped the weak force. Never for long, always on a tiny scale – because they lived in a universe ruled by the strong force.

The universe is dreamed by the void. It is made out of . . . grains of choice. Grains of virtual existence.

(Yes, *now* you're beginning to see.)

These basic grains are . . . *electons*. They elect their state of being.

Now look closer. Electons are really tiny dots, consisting of a circle of *Ka*-space rolled up compactly. Forever they unroll back into the void. Forever other bits of void roll up to replace them exactly. Roll up, roll up! Thanks to the

130

pressure of public opinion in the neighbourhood, the new electons choose to be just the same as the old ones.

All these electons roll-up compactly in the same direction. Thus time flows in one direction, in the universe. In *Ka*-space the electons aren't rolled up. So there in the never-ever all time is one, and timeless.

A mind, a *Ka*, must be a mesh of electons which are only partly rolled-up. Thus minds delve into time-past, into memory. Minds resist the flow of time.

That must be why old folk say that time speeds up as you grow older. The more you know and remember, the more your *Ka* resists. A fish washed along by a stream hardly seems – from the fish's point of view – to be moving at all. A fish swimming against the stream sees the water rush by on all sides . . .

Each death, each disappearance into *Ka*-space, removes a fraction of resistance. The forces balance again quickly. New *Ka*s come into existence.

What sort of shock would the death of almost all the minds in the galaxy deal to reality?

Enough to cause a lurch, a melting, a possible re-ordering of things?

Enough to bring about mastery of time – and mastery of Being – locally, for a few crucial moments?

The Godmind must think so.

Meanwhile your ship of *Ka*-space sails the void.

Could it explore many routes at once? Routes which would be real for a while; and then, not real? Many routes – which would later collapse into the one-and-only?

En route from Earth's Moon, once upon a time, the void bubbled and almost trapped you. You leapt out of that trap, into Narya's new-born body. Now you can escape any trap by shifting cabins within your many-chambered *Ka*-ship.

Find the place where that happened before!

Though it isn't one place. It's everywhere, anywhere.

Summon up a tapestry! And shift!

Yaleen! (A distraught cry in the distance.)

You goofed, Worm!

Summon another! Shift again.

Cross leagues of river	*This waterworld of isles*
By balloon	*And seas*
Beneath a Californian moon	*Where* Crackerjill
In darkness	*Flags down a breeze*
At the height of noon!	*And deserts into icecaps freeze!*

Worm-	*Papa's*	*Worm-*	*Cognizers*
Stranger	*Weight*	*Friend*	*Brood*
Tell of	*Will soon*	*To Ocean's*	*Where you*
Danger . . .	*Abate . . .*	*End . . .*	*Intrude . . .*

Suddenly you're in a body. As before it isn't yours to operate; you're only along for the ride . . .

. . . aboard a boat! Spray flies blindingly. Sails boom and clap. The deck pitches and rears. Through the yowling squall voices scream:

'Get to the lee of Rokka!'

'No, outrun! If them round north, them'll cut us!'

'Us could double.'

'Into *this*? You're mad. Outrun, I say!'

The mainmast creaks and groans as it leans this way, that way. Halyards crackle like whips. Figures in leathern cloaks haul themselves along the handrails.

And you? You're hunched in a wooden cage. One of your ankles is shackled with rusty iron to a bar. You're barefoot. Your torn linen gown is sodden. The cage is roped to belaying cleats, yet it still lurches to and fro on the slippery planking.

More figures loom. 'It's she as them want. Toss she overboard, cage an' all!'

'Naw. Them want we too.'

'Them might drop sails, try an' pick she up.'

'Cage 'ud break in that swell. Them never see.'

'God's mind! Try it, man!'

'Naw. Soon be in clean water. Just think how wor vicars shall smile when us turn up with a blackmind infanta. En't been a good torment on Soltrey since last all-eclipse. Them shall forgive us wor fines, eh?'

Bloody damn. You've been dumped in deep dung. This must be the waterworld of islands, all right, where the Godmind's good folk struggle against an evil worm. And no doubt it was predictable that you'd end up sharing minds with someone belonging to worm territory. Did she *have* to be a prisoner, caged, in the teeth of a storm, bound for torment?

Probably. Probably that put the worm uppermost in her mind. Probably her mind was naked to terror and desperate hope.

You're watching through her eyes. You're hearing through her ears. At least you aren't feeling the sting of the spray or the soak of her clothes.

So if she *is* tossed overboard, you personally won't have to endure choking. Or if she's delivered into the hands of their 'vicars' you yourself won't have to be cooked alive, or stretched, or whatever's planned. Presumably.

Why complain? Quite the home from home, all things considered! Here's a boat, right? (Though on what wild wide water, in what vile weather!) Here are more sodding swinish Sons, or the local equivalent.

Hey, *men* are sailing this vessel. Men.

Don't assume that everything's the same!

Make contact with your hostess. Find out what's what.

Hullo there.

Sweet Lordevil! Tis you! Save your servant! Oh Lordevil, you've come.

Sorry, but I'm not what's-his-name. My name's Yaleen. Is Lord of Evil what you call your worm?

Worm? What's this?

Is that what you call your sea-worm? Your black current?

Lordevil, don't mock when I need you so.

Hmm, this'll take a bit of explaining. I'm Yaleen, right? What's your name?

You know me, Lordevil!

I don't – honest. I'm just visiting. But I do have an urgent message for Lordevil, if Lordevil's who I think it is.

My black name's known only to you, Lordevil! Why do you not know it? Are you 'rasing me early, before the pains? Please call me by my black name.

Sorry, I don't know what a black name is. How about telling me your, um, white name?

Tisn't my blame they took me!

Of course not. They probably wanted lessons in elocution. Look, let's start again?

A wave breaks from starboard and sloshes right through the cage, battering it about. The ropes wrench but they hold.

Take me, Lordevil! Set me free! Or begging your pardon, it shall be too late. Turmoil's easing.

You could have fooled me.

No! Tisn't even tempest, this. Sky's breaking clear.

She could be right. There's a definite distinction between sea and sky ahead.

There's still the last wave, Lord! Tis skerry moil, this. There shall be the Mountain, yet.

If the storm's easing, your friends might catch us. They're chasing, right?

They shall quit at the edge of empty sea! You know that! And if they do overhaul before and these vicars' lice barter me, in their eyes mine's the blame; though it shan't cost my skin flayed cruel on Soltrey, only my having to be . . . but you know.

I keep telling you I don't.

You shall make me tell, still hoping for your help?

Yes, tell.

Why, I shall be anyone's bugger-butt, shan't I be?

Sounds disgusting. Say no more. Er, just how do you expect me to help? If I'm Lordevil, what form do I take on this planet?

You ask that? You can't be my Lord! You're personating!

I did just tell you my name's Yaleen, not Lordevil.

You're from the vicars' Godmind!

I'm bloody not. I'm from another planet. I'm waging war on the Godmind – and I want an alliance with your Lordevil!

Tis coming.

Lordevil's coming?

The Mountain comes!

As my hostess stares between the bars, the boat leans over and slides downhill into a sea-valley. A hill of water looms. Mountains on this world can't be enormous – not a patch on the Far Precipices – but the onrushing mass is still noteworthy.

''Ware! 'Ware tall water!''

Sailors in their leathern cloaks cling tight to any handy-hold; but your hostess hurls herself wildly from side to side, adding impetus to the slitherings of the cage. The mighty wave heaves the boat up high, askew. The spray-whipped cage slews violently. Tethers wrench at wooden bars. One bar snaps jaggedly. Rope snakes away. Cage spins, ripping free of other tethers. It's loose! It skids down the slanting deck; crashes into a rail. More bars splinter. Rail lurches outward.

Already the deck is righting itself; the cage hasn't managed to fall overboard. Your hostess wrestles frantically. Your shackle is free! You claw and heave, careless of any hurt. You ram your body through broken bars.

''Ware, captive!'

'Stop she!'

As the boat swings back, the hull becomes a steep and soaking hillside. Boulders of water pile at the bottom, crashing and splitting. There's no waiting! You slide headfirst down the timbers into the avalanching sea.

And under, and away.

You're upside-down. Twisted about. Rocks of water crush and pummel. Spew you up, drag you down. If the whole boat rolled over on you, you'd hardly know the difference.

Now and then your head breaks surface. You grab air. Air and water are so much churned together that hard knobs of sea burn in your sinuses, lodge in your lungs like stones.

Amazingly a barrel bobs by. With hoops of rope attached. Your spray-blind eyes nearly miss it. Blink, blink to see! Your fingers catch hold. Your clutch tight – and wretch liquid fire-stones from your chest and skull.

A rope drags across the clashing waves. A high hull grinds by, darkly. But from which boat does this life-rope hang? Is it from Bark's, or Soltrey's?

Abandon barrel. Catch rope. Hang on.

Papa's	'Hea-----ve-------ho!'
Weight	Slow voice, slurred and blurred.
Will soon	Gradually the crushing weight lessens.
Abate	Air can enter. Light, and life.
	The mountain rolls aside.

Revealing Shooshi! And – 'Looks like we're in time!' – Zelya; hovering over you in the palace of the time rites. The mountain is, of course, Mardoluc.

You're sitting up, gasping, grabbing air. How can you manage to sit up, or grab anything? It's far too sudden. Credence is nowhere in sight. 'Where is she? Where's Credence?' Shooshi and Zelya flutter hands in consternation. ('. . . only *pretending* timestop?' 'Impossible, Shooshoo!') Everyone else who was in a trance is still in a trance. Frozen lovers in the cushion pits, kneelers, hunchers. Peli down on her butt watching time-slowed ecstasy. Peera-pa just next to you, holding nobody's hands in hers. Not you: You're up. You're dancing with impatience. Shooshi and Zelya are gabbling and darting around.

'Stop it!' you shriek.

And still you speed up. Not just you – *everything else* as well! This isn't how it was when Marcialla speeded up. It's the whole world that's racing now. You can't follow what you're doing, you're doing things so fast. So who's doing them? You can't follow what the monitors are doing. You can't follow what they're saying, in their high-pitched squeaky voices. You can't follow what you're saying, yourself. So who's speaking?

Oh the wild onward rush of light and sound and action!

Weren't you supposed to be dead? Weren't you meant to be somewhere else? Wasn't there something about cabins in a ghostly galleon?

Ghostly is the world. Life is a fleeting wraith. Shadow and sun, places and people flicker wildly by . . .

It was the boat from your home isle of Bark which rescued you. That's weeks gone by, and now you and your hostess know each other rather better . . .

Her name is Infanta Farsi-podwy-fey, though you call her Pod for short. That's her 'sunshine name', the name by which she's known to family and acquaintances. Actually the 'farsi' and 'fey' bits of her name are titles, descriptions. Pod sees fleeting glimpses of events happening far away on her waterworld; that's *farsi*. She has an instinct for when people are about to die; that's *fey*. The 'infanta' part means that she's an unwed talent of Bark.

Pod also possesses a 'black name'. A person keeps their black name private, telling no one. The black name is a talent's power-name: the name which summons their power. If a stranger learnt it he might gain power over her. Or so they fancy, on Bark! The black name comes to a talented person in their dreams; and those dreams are sent by the worm of their world to all talents who inhabit isles in the great 'blackwaters' region – sent by Lordevil.

Some talents on Bark can envision far-scenes more vividly than Pod. Some can heal the sick, or sicken the healthy. Others can pick up lightweight objects with the force of their minds – or even project convincing illusions of simple objects such as chairs or vases. Pod's talents aren't outstanding; though at least she has them, which makes her an infanta.

Alas, the isle of Bark is right on the very periphery of Lordevil's influence. His ink stains the waters only thinly in this region. Five hundred sea-miles further west, in the heart of Lordevil's Dark, talents are much more powerful and dramatic. You find wizards and sorcerers.

It's true that such talents remain a minority of the total population throughout Lordevil's Dark. But where the seas are darkest – glossiest with Lordevil's presence – there's more power. A wizard who sails out from one of the central isles to somewhere like Bark loses some of his power; though he would still be a more potent wizard than any of the Barkish.

Obviously these talents are genetic – whatever Pod supposes about them being linked to eclipses of the various suns and moons. Just as obviously it was the urgent screaming need in her which drew you to share with her mind, rather than with some major sorceress of the inner Dark; with whom you might have been far better placed to contact Lordevil.

So here you are on Bark, instead. The isle is shaped like the skull of a hound: jaws agape, skerries for teeth, two freshwater lakes filling the eye sockets. Here you are in rocky Bark town, built on the steep brow frowning over the lake called Stare. (Of *stairs*, carved in rock, there are enough in this town to trump Verrino twice over in up-and-downness.)

More specifically, here you are ensconced in the Infantry of the Duenna; whence Pod slipped away, up and over the brow and down to the sea-shore on a mischievous cockle picnic – only to be waylaid and kidnapped by those uncouth pirates of Soltrey.

Luckily she jumped bravely overboard; so the Duenna frowns, but she hasn't decreed Pod's public humiliation. Whether Pod will now be traded westward, deeper into Lordevil's Dark, well-dowered by Barkish standards and in exchange for a dowerless maid of stronger talent who can breed Wizz-brats on Bark, remains a moot point.

(This whole business of trading maids is something to which *you* take considerable exception! Pod can't understand what you're rabbiting on about; so you've rather given up on the propaganda. As Pod sees it, how else could talent be improved out on the fringes? How else could powers best be stirred, so as to flow in a current, in and out?

(Why not trade stud-boys instead, say you!)

Here you are, looking from a stone casement down over roofs and stairs – and over Lake Stare – on a morn when Bigmoon is eclipsing Blindspot, sending temporary shadow across the town.

Blindspot is the sun which you don't even *glance* at if you value your eyesight. It's tiny and intensely bright – though its light isn't steady, more like a mirror flashing, flashing fast. There's also the giant sun Redfog, which is currently approaching hidden Blindspot; and elsewhere in the sky is the more sensible, yellow Homesun.

Moons also come in three sizes: Bigmoon, Midmoon and Baberock.

So Lordevil is spread throughout the blackwaters region, eh Pod? But he can clump together and rise up anywhere? In the sea off Bark, for instance?

He never has. That was desperate wishful thinking on my part – hoping he might somehow save me from the louts' ship. There isn't enough of him here at his edge.

Hmm. And Lordevil gathers in the Kas of the dead? So that they can relive their lives in the Lord for ever after?

Oh no. I hardly think so! When people of the dark waters die, Lordevil sucks back the powers he gave them – and he sends those powers forth to young new talents. Now do you understand?

Yes. Lordevil is kin to the black current of my own world. Obviously Lordevil stores Kas, the way those 'lectric batteries on Earth store power. He must have been dumped here once to soak up any native talent that emerged. Now he's gone his own way. He can make certain people in his domain powerful. And

140

the goodfolk of the clean water hate him deadly. Does Lordevil understand what he is? Do you, Pod? Does anyone?

Some of the Wizzes of Omphalos may. I once farsaw a Wizz communing with Lordevil. It was just a glimpse, quick as a Blindspot flash.

You must get yourself traded to Omphalos!

I thought you were opposed to that sort of thing?

I am. But you must.

What, me? A half-baked farsi-fey from a jewel-less isle on the very verge?

'Look, they're coming,' she says aloud.

Way below, four men who are wearing great white bone-combs in their oiled black hair are escorting a bald young woman, whose face is painted orange, up Plunge Stair. Those are the talent-traders from Tusk, a hundred sea-miles inward, accompanying their merchandise.

If only you could demonstrate a new talent, Pod!

I can't even show much farsi. As for fey, why fair enough if one of them's about to die! Which should make him very happy, I'm sure! The seer amongst them shall hear my Duenna's affidavit and shall peep me, and that shall be it. That's supposing I didn't throw all my chances away when those Vicars' lice took me.

Your Duenna said you were brave and adroit to get away into the waves.

Oh to save face she said it.

What if you could astonish the seer?

They should re-trade me further inward. Fat chance!

I'm with you, Pod. Maybe he could peep me.

You aren't talent, Yaleen. You're only a visitor squatting in me.

All the things I could tell you, to tell him!

So? He should have to peep them for himself.

(So . . . sew. *Sew* tapestries! You'd almost forgotten

141

about those other cabins! Is it possible to show their tapestries?)

Listen, Pod: I'm many persons. Each of me weaves her own vision. I want you to try as hard as you can to farsee my other selves. Your talents spring from Ka-*space – that's the key to my other cabins.*

I don't understand.

Let the seer peep tapestries of other worlds. You'll be the farsi who sees furthest of all! Try it! Together we'll get to Omphalos.

A distant bell begins to dong, summoning Pod and other infantas to the deep-hewn rock-room called Cave of Scales, where fates are weighed and talents are traded.

The walls of the Cave of Scales are scalloped by the chisels of long-dead stonemasons. The main body of the rock-room is a dome. Four subsidiary cupolas sprawl like paws. Two rock-shafts are the eye sockets of the room. By now Bigmoon has shifted aside from Brightspot, and Redfog is starting to eclipse the white dazzle; the light admitted down those shafts grows golden, amber. You're inside the shell of some great armoured beast eaten hollow by ants; only its corset of scales remaining.

Beneath one of the cupolas is a stone block whereon stand weighing pans of copper – a more obvious kind of Scales. (As so often on Bark, there are two levels of meaning. One is insufficient.) Both pans are piled with Barkish treasure – since you could hardly fit a talented maid into either of those pans, and if you did, it would likely bankrupt Bark to balance her weight. A relatively humble dowry is on show, though displayed to best effect. There are well-sheened nacre shells, goblets of volcano-glass, jars of seacumber salve, a conch-trumpet with silver clasps.

Candidate infantas occupy benches beneath the second

cupola. Under the third cupola, alone on a low stool, sits the young woman with shaved head and orange face. She looks disdainfully amused by her out-isle cousins. The fourth cupola shelters her escort of talent-traders. Centre stage – the dome itself – is occupied by the Duenna, her face and figure enveloped in black fish-net garb.

'Farsi-podwy-fey,' creaks her voice. Now it's Pod's turn to show off her wares.

As Pod rises and advances, the seer from Tusk adopts a poised, intent stance.

Now, Pod!

Pod whispers her black name to herself in an undervoice which you cannot hear.

Shift! Shift cabins in your ship of *Ka*-space. Linger. And while you linger, a sister of yours shares Pod's mind. Shift back.

Yes?

Oh yes.

Pod farsaw a tapestry of bile-green swamp and silt isles. A honeycombed cliff reared high. She hung frozen on a breeze: birdwoman. Suddenly the woven threads had writhed into reality. She plummeted, to snatch a swimming snake . . . It was Marl's world.

Shift! Linger. Shift back.

This time Pod farsaw a world of yellow clay, flat as a platter. Several great globular vegetables, crowned with horny leaves, broke the monotony; also a pear-shaped plant, its midriff plated with stiff leaves. From the top of this pear rose a thin erect stalk like a root tapping the air. In the crown of the pear three hauntingly human eyes stared fixedly ahead. Energy crackled in a cloudless eggshell sky. Stabs of lightning slashed at one another . . .

The seer, astonished, kneels before Pod.

* * *

With a lurch, the flickering lights and shadows slow abruptly . . .

Oh wasn't Donnah furious when you and Peli got back aboard the *Crackerjill* after your truant trip to the temple! That's when she muttered darkly, 'Just you wait, little priestess. Just you wait.'

Wait for what?

Wait for weeks. Weeks while your priestess's progress took you onward to Tambimatu. Weeks more while *Crackerjill* sailed back north again.

On the return voyage *Crackerjill* only called in quickly at the towns en route: barely half a day in port to stock up on fresh fruit and veg, and no stopover whatever at Port Barbra. Presently you docked at smoky Guineamoy.

Fortunately it's wintertime, so you don't have to open the port for ventilation; the outside air is none too sweet. (To the people of Guineamoy, does the air of other towns smell wild and raw, uncivilized?) Through the glass port, in the grey sky over the town, you can watch a huge balloon blundering through its paces . . .

You can. You.

This is the weirdest thing. Many weeks have flown by at utmost speed, far too fast for you to notice anything beyond the rushing and the flickering, the tick-tock rhythm of day and night. You can't say you've 'lived' through those weeks. Yet now that time has suddenly resumed its normal pace, you can recall everything that happened in the interval, just as though you'd been a conscious part of everything that occurred.

You've been part of a living tapestry. One which alters and evolves. One which shows you what will happen if you start from such and such a point, and move in a certain direction. Why, after a while you must reach Guineamoy.

144

'Yal-eeeen!' Boots bash along the corridor. The cabin door wrenches open. Donnah bursts in.

'Why, you little – !' She's livid with anger. She brandishes papers, pages of newssheet.

'*This* is on sale all over town!' She thrusts what she's clutching under your nose.

It's *The Book of the Stars* by Yaleen of Pecawar, printed in neat columns on big smudgy sheets of newsprint. Of course. What else?

'Right here in Guineamoy, where we've had the most trouble persuading people to take their medicine!'

'Good. Maybe this'll do the job better.'

'Will it really? Well I'll have you know that I've sent urgent signals north and south.'

'What for?'

'To search all cargoes, dear girl! To intercept the rest of these.'

Should you tell her the truth about the way your book has been published? Should you keep mum about it? Which?

The entire boat trembles. The cabin and Donnah are suddenly double before your eyes. Two Donnahs, two cabins occupy the same space, superimposed. In one of these cabins you tell Donnah. In the other you don't tell. Whole tableaus of ghost events weave forth from this moment, till whenever.

Donnah steps back and sneers. 'That'll settle you, my child. Don't think we can't manage to contain this. Difficult, I admit! But possible. Possible indeed.'

'You could have saved yourself the bother of signalling, Donnah.'

'Oh really? This certainly wasn't on sale in Spanglestream a few days back. And we haven't received any signals from Gate of the South, have we? I presume it appealed to your sense of vanity to have this thing published just as you arrived in town.'

'Wrong. It's on sale everywhere from Tambimatu to Umdala. Simultaneous release, today.' (At least you hope so.) 'It's a fate accomplished, Donnah, that's what it is. A fate accomplished. But don't *worry*. The book won't do any harm. Only good. If good can be done.'

'I see.' There's great restraint in her voice. But not in her hands. She hurls the sheets of the book at you; though since these are loose they simply unfurl and flutter variously to the floor. '*Yours*, I believe. May a drunken spider have misprinted everything.'

You recover a sheet. 'Looks okay to me.'

'Oh, *by* the way.' Donnah pauses at the door. 'I believe the guild will now wish to shift the current further north – before anyone hatches fancy ideas of exporting your words to the Sons, for their salvation.'

'But . . . but what about all that land that'll be left vacant over there? After the Sons get brainburnt? I thought your plan was . . . I mean, if you completely block passage over the river . . .'

'Look out that port. Balloons are coming along famously here. On a calm day it shouldn't take much power to push really big passenger balloons across the river, nice and high above the current. Balloons crammed with colonists, eh?'

'Oh.'

'Ever had a hankering to sail the wild ocean, in a Worm's wide mouth?'

'I shan't do it.'

'*I* wouldn't force you. That's the honest truth. You know how much it appalled me when your boyfriend Tam lost one of his hands. But I'm not in Pecawar, where Tam is. Where your dad is. Both of them within a stone's throw of Quaymistress Chanoose! Chanoose is a ruthless character; be warned.'

'That's how things stand, is it?'

'I wouldn't say they stand this way; or that way. I'm simply speculating.'

'That's a pretty poisonous speculation.'

'Blame the Sons for poisoning us.'

'It's foul! Don't ever bother washing, Donnah. You can't cleanse yourself. You smell – *inside*.'

'Ho, ho; now the little innocent speaks of cleanliness, after spreading that document across the land without permission.'

'I only needed my *own* permission.'

'Did you? Why, in that case maybe anything is permitted to anybody to achieve what they want. Sauce for the goose, Yaleen!'

'Um . . . how would I get back from the ocean?'

'Nothing simpler. The Worm gulps you down, and wriggles you back through its body – to some agreed pick-up point, hmm? Fate accomplished, Yaleen! Yours. Most likely.'

Everything rushes into a blur.

It's been a good few bigmonths, many midmonths and lots of babemonths since you and Pod set out from Bark, escorted by those Tuskish traders with the bone-combs in their hair. Everything has taken far too long.

At last you're on the isle of Omphalos. This island is a ring of hills lapped by the black sea. Set on the tips of the crags are the keeps of the Wizzes. In the broad bowl of valley within, are farms, forests, lakes of flying fowl – and a town called Tomf. The name Tomf sounds like the dull throb of a giant kettledrum. Imagine vellum stretched from crag to crag across the fertile cauldron of the valley.

Consider the homes of the Wizzes as drum-screws. Sometimes the most powerful Wizzes play strange music upon Tomf from their heights.

How soon will Yaleen destroy the Godmind's rose garden on the Moon?

How soon will the Godmind decide that Project Mindburner might just as well commence?

Soon, perhaps.

'Infanta Farsi! Redfog eclipses Blindspot! Tis time to leave the inn!'

Check your orange-painted face one last time in the brass-framed mirror. Make haste. Unlatch the door. Your talent-trader, Seer Makko, awaits.

His hair is freshly oiled and his comb poised jauntily. He sketches a quick bow, casual, almost affectionate. This man of Tusk respects you, wonders at you. During the long voyage of many landfalls you have, what's more, become his friend.

His strongman, Innocence, lingers further along the buckled wooden corridor; knife tucked in his belt, sack slung over his shoulder containing your portion of the treasure dowry of Bark. Pod, who farsees distant worlds, is her own treasure by now. She is a veritable Princess of Talents. So perhaps her dowry has come to seem excessive, albeit no jewels are included. Half a dozen gingerworms wrapped in a leaf might be more suitable. Yet since the traders set out with that sack, deliver it they must.

'We must hasten, 'Fanta!'

Along the corridor. Down squeaking stairs. Into the flaking whitewashed vestibule betwixt boozery and kitchen where Mistress Umdik presides – 'Mild days, Mistress!' 'Mild days, Sirs and 'Fanta!' – and out on to the cobbled thoroughfare.

Already, as Blindspot shines through the fringe of

Redfog, the street of timbered houses is gilded. By the time you reach the marriage mart the daylight will be full orange. *No one gets hoodwinked when Blindspot hides*; so goes the saying. During Blindspot's eclipse a person can look everywhere, consider all aspects of a bargain. Indeed you could even glance directly at Blindspot, masked as it is by Redfog, transfiguring Redfog into a huge glowing fruit in the sky; though no one would dream of such rashness.

Up Stargazy Road you go. Across the Avenue of Heartchoke, and you're there.

The marriage mart itself is a white dome set on pillars in the midst of Omblik Square. Omblik Square is where the blackfish vendors usually sell the fruits of the sea, kept fresh in all manner of tanks: tanks made of glass, of stone, of caulked wood, of canvas. Today only the permanent tanks are present, some brimful, some empty; some pure, some rank. No vendors; not of fish, at least.

Soon you're moving amongst infantas of other isles accompanied by their traders. Some wear silken saris – of purple, pink and patchwork – far more elegant than Pod's kirtle, shirt and plaid. Nobles and humbles of Omphalos circulate and chatter and assess; any of whom is more richly robed than the most princely person on Bark. Already dowries are set out on tables; Innocence hastens to set out Pod's. Some dowries are splendid indeed; perhaps the infantas in question are poor in talent. Perhaps where these infantas come from such a heap of riches is considered a humble dowry fit for a powerful talent.

Redfog burns orange in the sky. The burly marriage mistress claps her hands; she wears a full black weed-veil set with sparklers, dropping down from the crown of her head to her toes.

'Because of extraordinary claims, I call first upon the Infanta Farsi-podwy, all the way from far Bark.'

'Claims!' mutters Makko. 'She insults you.'

'She left out the last part of my title!'

'If the Infanta hides as huge a talent as we've heard,' continues the veiled woman, 'why does she not bless the outer isles with herself? So that we can balance and build our abilities throughout all of Lordevil's Dark?'

'I'm she,' Pod calls out, 'and I shall only wed a Wizz. None less. Together we shall speak to the stars. Tis why I'm here.'

'Your traders have voiced it about that you shall only wed a Wizz – but has any Wizz heard this?'

'Yes indeed,' calls a tall slim handsome fellow. A cloak, clasped at his throat with a golden buckle, swirls about him as he forges through the crowd. On his head he wears a slouch hat with tail feathers of fowls sticking out behind like the rudder on a windmill.

'You, sir?' The veiled woman's tone is hesitant, shy.

The tall man doffs his hat and bows. For a moment or two, while his hat is off, he flickers and is someone else: someone old and small and chubby with a mischievous smile. As soon as he resumes his hat, he appears as he was before.

'Ah!' Makko murmurs into Pod's ear, 'It's a master of illusions! If he takes to you, he shall pay me well for my work.'

The man's eyes bore into Pod's, piercing any illusions she herself may have.

Farsee, Pod! Farsee!

(Shift! Shift!)

Briefly puzzlement is writ on the master's face. Soon, fascination – and bewitchment.

With a jolt, the world slows. Other fiercer jolts continue. The Worm has left Umdala far behind; Umdala with its

150

geometric rows of blockhouses, Umdala with its estuarine marshes. Onward, northward, the Worm courses, smashing through ever more swelling waves which are whipped by wind and ocean width and by the torque of the world, as the estuary widens out into the wild dire salty seas where no one ever dare sail.

Spray drenches you, girl, as you crouch in the Worm's maw, wretched, on the point of puking.

And you remember: how long it took you to arrive here. How long, since Guineamoy. How the tapestry has evolved meanwhile.

The waves jog other knowledge too: knowledge of a wild storm on a waterworld of islands many 'months' ago.

Where does this knowledge come from?

Worm?

What?

I'm some place else, as well as here! I'm in many places! You tried to kill me in the time temple. No, that's wrong! You did kill me. What's happening now is what would have happened, if you hadn't killed me. It's what-was-possible. It's happening just as if it's real.

Oh what a potent potentiality this is! It could become real indeed. You're sure of it. But then, what price your other selves? Would they be lost? Would you be lost?

Are you feeling okay, Yaleen?

Of course I'm not! I feel like spewing my guts all over you.

Not much of a sailor, are we?

This isn't sailing. This is lunacy. How much further?

Just till I reach where I was formerly. Soon, soon.

The Worm's head rolls through a hill of water. Spray smashes into the open jaws.

Of a sudden, the onward motion ceases. The Worm lolls.

Have we arrived?

Yaleen! It's starting! Mindburner's starting! Oh the light, intolerable light! Oh the dying! The lens of Kas is forming. Oh the power — it's sweeping all the stars. I can't shelter, can't protect — !

Worm?

A scream in the mind.

Escape! Track back. Shift, shift!

Mount Mardoluc, in falling upon you, broke your leg. You stayed on at the temple, scoffing gourmet meals while your bone mended. Peli also stayed. Credence made her peace with you.

Then you stayed on some more, really getting yourself involved in the synchronous rite and the periodic rite. By the time *The Book of the Stars* was in print everywhere, you were too deep into the rites of Being to tear yourself away. Besides, the river guild would dearly have loved to lay their hands on you.

Some tens of weeks later, while you're en-tranced in the synchronous rite, Mindburner strikes . . .

Shooshi and Zelya saved you from suffocation; and Credence fled. She jogged back to 'Barbra. To win her way into the favours of the river guild, she not only told where you were — she betrayed the whole scheme to distribute *The Book of the Stars* secretly everywhere from Tambimatu to Umdala.

A runner arrived with a warning, not far ahead of Donnah's guards. You fled the temple, with Peli and Peerapa. Papa, of course, couldn't flee. By forest and jungle ways you fled, ending up at last with friends of the 'Barbra cultists in Ajelobo.

Donnah burnt down the glorious secret temple; so an

Ajelobo newssheet reports. The story doesn't say whether Papa Mardoluc was inside at the time . . .

You didn't open your big mouth to boast, aboard the *Crackerjill* docked at Guineamoy. You blamed Stamno the renegade for the publication. You blamed the river guild for bringing him to Pecawar to corrupt you. You were shocked. You bitterly regretted. Donnah believed you.

In the end Mindburner comes. When the Worm is quenched and wrenched through time and space, your shield is gone.

And the Godmind slays you impersonally. Not even in revenge for blighted roses. More like piranha-mice on the rampage, hungry for every last living morsel . . .

You stand atop the Spire at Verrino, looking down upon town and river, remembering your first view of this vista.

Suddenly, there appears below you the bowl of a valley instead. Farms, forests, lakes of flying fowl, and a strange town (yet not so strange) – all enclosed by a great rim of crags.

One tiny fierce sun glares through a second foggy red sun, like a life-seed incandescent in the yolk of an egg. The seed is near the edge of the yolk. There's also a third sun, mellow yellow. A moon of bone shares the sky.

An inner light blinds the universe. A worm writhes and withers. Mindburner!

'And as my wedding gift to you, dear Podwy,' the small chubby old man promises, 'I shall weave the grandest of all illusions!'

You're on the topmost platform of Master Aldino's tower. Flagstones spiral outward from an open stairwell, each flag painted with a different faint and flaking but still potent symbol, work of the previous owner. The circuit wall is a shade too low for comfort. It's barely waist-high. Immediately below, there's turf. Then jagged crags drop away. On the north side of the tower these dive down to the black sea. Southward, they tumble into the valley. To east and west the chain of hills strides away. This keep is poised on the sharpest ridge of all, as if balanced on an axe blade.

A path winds steeply down the south face; none down the north face. Omphalos harbour lies far away, beyond the softer southern crags.

As hat, the tower wears a cone of wood on stilts. A system of gutters pipes rainwater down into tanks on the floor below. One of these tanks is heated – spasmodically, clouds permitting – by a mirror contraption jutting from the wall, which by means of clockwork follows the path of Homesun to concentrate its rays. Thus there is hot and cold running water in the living quarters, gravity-fed from overhead. This is only one of the ingenious comforts. As a home, the keep isn't to be sniffed at; though admittedly it's a strenuous climb down to the valley and back to fetch groceries. If the crags were a bit nearer vertical, a bucket on the end of a rope mightn't be a bad idea. Two other wives already reside in the keep, along with a number of servant lads – potential Wizzes. So there's company, besides Aldino's.

He gestures grandly across the valley, almost overbalancing. 'This afternoon, yon vale of Omphalos shall wear any guise you choose. Um, within reason.'

And tonight, in the bedchamber, shall he don his best illusory body in Pod's honour?

So long as old Aldy isn't too drunk to concentrate (said senior wife Lotja, teasing – or bitching).

'Choose, my dear! Choose one of those other worlds

154

which you farsee! We shall let the good folk of Tomf wend their way for an hour or so bemused through alien thoroughfares. Um, I hope no other Big Wizz gets annoyed. Still, why should they? We're all friends, after a fashion. It's my third wedding day. Licence is allowed.'

'Shall other Wizzes be coming as guests?'

'Perhaps some shall peep in, from far.' Aldino's finger wavers about till he locates the fretted bump of another keep away to the east. 'Perhaps Master Airshoe shall float over. Let's hope he doesn't bother. Has an eye for my Lotja, does Master Airshoe; and this evening I shall have my attention diverted, eh Podwy?'

Time to prompt Pod.

'Do tell me, Master, how do you manage to weave such wonderful illusions for all to see?'

'Um. Well, let me see. Waves of energy are forever rebounding off the world. Some of these waves – only a few, mark you, out of many – pass through the windows of your eyes. Right? So already you're gathering in just one aspect of a reflection. What's more, your eyes don't actually see. They simply gather the waves. When those waves wash against the back of the eye, echoes are made. And those echoes of an aspect of a reflection travel onward into your head.'

He taps his balding pate. 'In here your brain dreams up images which it believes to correspond to those echoes. By now you're at four removes from reality. Count them: image, echo, aspect, reflection. What I do is reverse this process. I imagine that I'm seeing something quite different, something I wish to see. I send out echoes of stronger, more potent aspects. Other folk in the neighbourhood reflect those echoes – and they dream that they see what I'm imagining.'

With that mischievous grin of his, he adds, 'Leastways,

that's what I *feel* that I'm doing, my dearest. That's the way I have to feel to accomplish illusions. Yet mayhap I'm really doing something entirely different! Mayhap what I've described is only the emblem which I show to myself, wherewith to unlock my magic.' He stabs a demonstrative finger at various symbols on the stone flags. 'An emblem such as those ones; though my own emblem is inscribed inside my head, out of sight. Of course, while doing all this I need to bless the name of Lordevil who empowers me.'

You confer with your hostess.

Pod says, 'Master Aldino, I've decided which world I wish to see spread across this vale.'

'Dino to you, dearest girl.' He pats and tweaks Pod's shoulder, where some flesh is exposed. 'Would you care to give me a teasing glimpse?'

Wedding hour. Homesun beams down. Blindspot burns through Redfog. Bigmoon is a faint white bone aloft.

Below in the living quarters a feast awaits: of spit-roast fowl, gingerworms baked in sweetcrust, pickled cumber, decapod claws, wrack cake, rasperry pud, ricewine.

Up atop the tower here, Lotja plays airs on her xithar whilst midwife Polloo chats to Master Airshoe who did indeed float over. He arrived on a fluffy little cloud of his own conjuring. When Airshoe walks on air, he prefers not to see too much empty space yawning beneath. He's a well-built fellow with a neatly jutting beard and a big tuberous nose. His lips are fat and juicy. Studiously ignoring Lotja for the nonce, he occupies himself with Polloo.

Plus several more guests; no doubt including some uninvited ones who aren't present in person, only in the mind's eye. However, the guest list shall shortly include every soul in Tomf, and in Omphalos valley too. Hand in hand with Pod, Aldino poses at the parapet. He looks outward. He breathes deeply. He looks inward.

Now, Pod! Farsee!

And shift!

Shift back.

Appears Verrino . . .

You're high atop the Spire (of course). Below in the vale is Verrino town, just as it was before the Sons trashed the place. No ash heaps or rubble. No broken windows; no smashed terracotta urns.

You can see all these details clearly, for Verrino town is magnified, enlarged. Verrino fills up half of Omphalos valley – surely Aldino got things out of proportion! Verrino isn't superimposed on Tomf, one to one. Tomf is totally submerged by the visionary city. Maybe a single Verrino plaza or wine-arbour holds the real Tomf hidden within. Far from having to blunder through the alien alleys of another world, the good folk of Tomf can only stare amazed at this city of giants which has suddenly sprung up, swallowing and dwarfing their mini-ville.

Where are the giant inhabitants? No one is about in Verrino. It must be very early morning.

Beyond Verrino, bends the river.

Ah, now you understand the workings of this vision. The whole vista is as if seen through the eye of a fish. Consequently the heart of Verrino town is enlarged, and fills up the foreground. At the outskirts it bends away, shrinking fast. The river also bends away, curving beside increasingly distorted shores. The whole illusion seems wrapped around a globe of air, or a balloon, which nestles in Omphalos vale.

The vision is how you imagine one of those goose eggs which Dario's brother said he painted; if instead of men's nude bodies curving around the shell you had a whole town and river, with the vale as the eggcup.

It's a circle of *Ka*-space, wrapped compactly around itself – writ large. It's an electon, hugely magnified.

The electon encloses a whole town. It could easily enclose an entire world. It's only a conjured illusion. *Or is it*?

'Bravo!' applauds Master Airshoe. Lotja riffs her xithar, repeating the same phrase a dozen times over.

'Your wedding gift, my dear,' puffs the proud conjuror.

'Oh Dino,' breathes Pod, 'for sure, you're the Wizz of Wizzes.'

And of course this vision of Verrino – and of the river bending away in the background – comes complete with a worm, thin as a thread upon the shrunken water, yet blackly visible.

'One more boon, husband-to-be! You bring me this vision through your skill – but also through the power of Lordevil, isn't that so? Shall you summon Lordevil himself? Shall you make our black lord manifest in some guise or other? If only as a voice in our midst! Let Lordevil bless our union personally.'

'Humph. Is that all? Perhaps you should also like Blind-spot as a brooch?'

'Oh Dino, do you mean you can't contact Lordevil?'

'Course you can,' chips in Master Airshoe. 'Big Wizz like you.'

'I shall tire myself. This is a conspiracy!'

'Nonsense, old friend. Shall I help? Shall we join forces? Do permit. Let this be my wedding gift to yourself and your beautiful bride.'

'Ach, you already have your eyes on her too! One of my wives isn't sufficient to seduce!'

Verrino flickers and wavers; then holds firm again.

'No such thing, old friend! Curb your wild suspicions.'

'Hrumph.'

'If that's what you suspect, shouldn't you prefer me to exhaust some of my – ha, ha – over-abundant energy?'

'That,' remarks Polloo, 'might be a good idea.' She eyes Lotja, who looks somewhat crestfallen and strums a discord.

'Oh very well. The two of us in concert. You take the lead, Airshoe. I shall sustain my vision. Though mayhap I should let it pop? Dear Podwy has already admired one marvel. Now she cries for stronger music and for madder wine.'

'No, no!' protests Pod. 'Sustain it. Please! It contains . . .'

'Contains what?'

'It contains an alien Lordevil, in that river there.'

'Does it indeed? Whatever makes you think so?'

'I, er . . .'

'Tell me, wife-to-be!'

'I'm, er, I'm carrying a passenger within me.'

'You're *pregnant*? Already? This wretched Airshoe only met you a moment ago!' Aldino's eyes widen. Again Verrino ripples. 'Was it your escort? That grasping talent-trader whom I paid so handsomely? Did he enjoy you on shipboard?'

'No, no, Dino, you misunderstand. I'm an honest virgin. My passenger is in my mind, not in my womb. She's from that city there below.'

I'm from Pecawar, Pod. But let's not split hairs.

'Podwy! Do you mean to tell me – *now*, five minutes into our nuptials – that you've been farseeing these alien worlds of yours not by virtue of your own talent, but courtesy of some infestatious visitor? One who might fly away again? Leaving you bereft of your farsi? Ach, I've been cheated!'

159

Pod is on the verge of weeping; you buoy her up. Pride flares; honour burns bright. 'Master Aldino, *sir*, I am the Infanta *Farsi*-podwy-*fey*, of Bark Isle! See within me what I am, and who is within me! See how great her mission is!'

'Farsi . . . courtesy of another! That's what I see. Oh what a blind old fool I've been. I'm gulled and flummoxed. What price your feyness? Is that a cheat too? Go on: fey something! I'll tell you what to fey. Fey yourself falling from these battlements, right soon!'

'*That*, I shan't permit,' declares Airshoe. 'I should hold her up.'

Lotja sniggers. Other guests studiously scrutinize the sky.

'Podwy! You shall fey *Airshoe* colliding with cliffs – when my illusions warp his knowing where he is!' Oh, Aldino is working himself up into a right old petulant lather. Verrino looks sadly tatty and wispy.

'Fey! Fey away! I'll bet you can't fey the death of a fly.'

Furious, Pod cried, 'I shall fey in truth! I feel the talent rising. I shall fey your own fate, sir, contemptuous husband.'

No, Pod. We're diving into deep manure. This is awful. I absolutely must contact Lordevil – while Verrino's still here, with my Worm. Cool it, will you?

However, Pod rises on tiptoe. 'I fey – !'

She screams.

Horror twists her face.

'I fey death! Death everywhere! The death of everyone! All the vicars of whitewater and all their Godmind flock, across the world – burnt up! Lordevil destroyed and changed a moment later! Every soul I've known on Bark. Everyone who's harboured in Lordevil's Dark. All the Wizzes and all the commons of Omphalos – brainburnt! And me, me too. A faggot to fuel a blaze.'

She sinks down, devastated. 'Oh I fey, I fey indeed. Never did I fey like this. I farsee-fey: death everywhere in all the stars. The finish of life. Lordevil's end. The stop of the whole world, and all worlds. All at once.'

How soon, Pod? How soon?

'As soon as Blindspot leaves Redfog. When Blindspot burns bright, we burn!'

'What's this?' a shocked Aldino asks.

Beg him to raise Lordevil, Pod. Quickly, do it quickly.

'Dino – husband – if you don't summon Lordevil, we're doomed. Even if you do, we're doomed – since I fey it so. I'm so scared. But do it, do it!'

Already the orange hue is lessening. Day is whitening again.

'What do you make of this, Airshoe?'

'I think, old friend, mayhap we should err on the side of credulity.'

'Believe her?'

'Exactly.'

Hurry, hurry!

Aldino and Airshoe link hands. They begin to leap up and down, jumping as they do so from one flagstone emblem to the next, panting rapidly, deliberately.

Day whitens.

An inner light dawns, such as no other light that ever was. The light blazes up in Pod's mind. The whole universe burns with it. The light is a vortex of brilliance, tearing her loose from herself, sucking her up towards . . .

. . . a pattern, a bright web which spans the shadows of the stars, the ghosts of all the worlds.

Recognize the pattern? How could you not? You've been well trained in the appreciation of it! It is a pattern of a hundred petals, unfolding across the galaxy, blooming fiercely. It is a cosmic rose. Each world is a petal. Each cell

161

in each petal is a *Ka*. And all of those petals focus *Ka*-light through the heart of the rose.

Yaleen has blasted the garden in the Moon. The God-mind has struck out. This is Mindburner.

But you're *already* dead.

Cognizers	The world's as flat as a pancake. Shabby
Brood	yellow. Colour of clay. Sometimes energies
Where you	discharge across the streaky sapphire sky.
Intrude	That's about it, by way of action. Otherwise
	night follows day follows night.

In fact it's hardly a world at all. It's just a flat surface, with length in one direction and breadth in the other. Life's hardly turbulent. Your hostess Hovarzu has stood in this same spot for the last five years. No doubt she could stand here for the next five.

Yet within her there is such richness and such depth. Abstract tapestries – models of the cosmos – beckon and glisten inside her. Many of these are strange and fanciful; others are rigorous and austere. It's these models that she strolls around in. She's good practice for if you ever break your back and have to spend the next ten years in bed.

Hovarzu used to be a friend of Ambroz, whom you met in Eeden. When he was alive they often talked by 'radio'. From her point of view he hasn't been dead and withered long at all. Ambroz was a disciple of old Harvaz the Cognizer; so too is plantlady Hovarzu. During your stay in her mind (which seems *interminable*) you've enriched her quite a lot. She has made new cosmic models and beamed these to other kindred cognoscenti amongst Cognizers.

Not all plant-people are Cognizers. Some make music in their minds. Some chant epic poems full of Earthmyth and anticipations of an afterlife when they will all stride freely forth, alien Aeneas and Achilles in the Champs Elysées.

162

Others ponder the varieties of infinity from the aspect of beauty. They classify the orders of magnitude aesthetically: the infinitesimal, the purely infinite, the set of sets, the alephs and omegas, the satori series. Still other plant-people tell the beads of the genes.

Not all Cognizers concern themselves with the methods and motives of the Godmind. But Ambroz did; and so does Hovarzu. That's why you vectored in on her; on account of the echoes you both share. So she tells you.

Hovarzu doesn't find it a weird experience to host you. She's used to radio-voices in her brain; to whole tapestries of thought being transmitted into her from a distance.

Lodger-within, let us consider Kas!

Yes, let's.

And dimensions; and electons.

Right!

After all this time you have a pretty good idea what Hovarzu looks like to an outsider; though it wasn't too easy to find out.

True, she keeps her three eyes open during the day. But that isn't so that she can admire the view – or keep tabs on her personal appearance. Her eyes, in common with her leaf-plates, are designed to drink light and turn it into energy. (If they weren't so designed, maybe she would shut her eyes and never bother to open them again, given the monotonous poverty of the view. Might this be the real reason why her eyes sup light? To keep her at least somewhat connected with the world around?)

A few other huge native vegetables break the uniformity of the plain. Some look like leeks carved of wood. Others resemble artichoke heads. But no other plant-person is in sight. That's why it took a while to work out Hovarzu's own design – a topic of little interest to her.

She resembles a very tough pear. Below her waist she's

skirted by leaf-plates which she can open and close. She's rooted by a trifork of toothed spade-roots, and a retractable tap-pipe runs down to the water table. (How you had to nag to garner this item!) It's upon those spades that she can waddle away, if she ever wishes to. A stalk rising from her head is her radio antenna. Her inner workings are a mystery.

So the universe is composed of electons, which are infinitesimal circles of Ka-space rolled up very compactly. That's so, Yaleen?

That's how it seemed.

And electons usually choose to be what they have always been. So reality recreates itself from moment to moment, from amidst a flux of options. This process is the breath of Being. But the world doesn't wink in and out of existence all together, on-off like a signal lamp. No! All of reality is forever winking in and out simultaneously. Thus reality sustains itself. There's always a familiar neighbourhood.

Makes sense!

Yet I believe that there are minor cycles within the breath of Being. By breathing in tune with these, the wizards of old Earth must have worked their temporary alterations of reality – if legend can be trusted. In addition there is also a Grand Rhythm, a Climacteric Rhythm – whereby large zones of reality eclipse in and out, restoring themselves exactly as before, unconsciously.

Could be. So where do Kas come into this?

Kas, Yaleen, must be dimension-fields of electons where the field itself is conscious. What happens, then, when true death arrives? Supposing that a Ka is not bound by a worm? Supposing that it is not drawn back into flesh by the Godmind? This is the great mystery. Perhaps the Kas of all those who are truly dead diffuse into the infinitude of Ka-space – where each contributes one more iota of will and awareness. Then one day in the distant future Ka-space will become fully conscious. It will be able consciously to project forth the universe that it chooses; not just the universe which happens to exist already.

Unless the Godmind gets there first.

The Godmind is a creation. It is not the Creating. Nevertheless its schemes are clever. If it succeeds in marshalling this cosmic lens of electons, it may discover how to control reality; how to become the guiding overseer. It may achieve this feat long before Ka-space evolves the capacity on its own account – from out of the stored will and awareness of all the dead. Then the Godmind will be a God indeed. Perhaps only the God of a single galaxy out of many million; but a God, even so.

But it'll have killed off everyone. What's the point in ruling a graveyard?

It may gain the power to recreate people! To restore their Kas to the flesh! As well as the power to twist the black currents back through time as destroyers of potential rivals! Consider the proposed act of mass murder further, Yaleen. The transfer of so many dimension-fields will send a shock through Ka-space and through the universe which it projects. Locally, at least, in this galaxy of ours. The breath of Being will break rhythm. Minor cycles will culminate. A Grand Climacteric will quake forth. This will –

Hovarzu?

The dazzling inner light! The deadly radiance!

Shift out! Shift out!

When you all shift at once, you all collide.

You, overlooking Omphalos, belly-button of Lordevil's Dark.

You, planted on a plain that's flat as a platter.

You, who've probed the secrets of the heartwood porter.

You, on another worm-world: one of volcanoes, rivers of fire, pools of liquid tin.

You, you, and you.

You, probably at Verrino.

You, potentially aboard the Worm's gob out in the wild ocean.

You, possibly engaged in the synchronous rite during timestop in the palace of enchantment.

You, you.

Cabins tumble into one another. Tapestries interweave. You

U-nite!

I . . .

I span the ghosts of stars. I grasp the rose . . .

. . . as the souls of the colonies, and of Earth and Luna too, are all sucked into *Ka*-space, shaking the ever-never fabric of the void . . .

. . . as the Godmind turns its lens of death upon Deeptime, upon distances so great that they aren't to be measured in millions of millions of leagues but only in aeons of aeons . . .

. . . all at once.

Ineffably swift, the lightflood pulses. Oh let me timestop it. Let me catch it on the hop. Oh yes.

The heart and lungs of Being beat and bellow. Let me lay my finger on that heart, let me collapse those lungs then kiss life into them again. Yes, oh!

I am here, I am everywhere, I am never-ever. I am the raven and the writing desk. I am she who was born and born again. I am she who twisted time. The radiance shines through me. I've captured the rose dynamic. I am the lens; I am the rose.

The Grand Climacteric is here, my darlings. The college of electons is in session, all of one accord at once.

Down there in the worlds of death, reality crackles like

166

ice. It melts, it flows. So many streams, so many branches! So infinite a pool of possibles. So many actuals, woven in my memories. Taught in timestop (thanks, Peepy!), taught in farsee (thanks, Pod!), taught in the mastery of illusions (thanks, Dino!), taught in the record of memory and in the shapes of power (thanks, Worm!), taught in the guile of shifting cabins (thanks, Credence!), taught in cognizing (thanks, Hovarzu!), taught many other precious things (thanks, whoever you are!); even so I cannot choose by thought and will. I can only let myself be chosen. I can only let myheartself, my wishself, be the new pattern. Melting, flowing; and in the moment of *I am*, refreezing . . .

. . . I am drawn down, descending with the rose.

PART FOUR
The Rose Balloon

Blood streamed through the sky over Manhome South. Scarlet gore flowed above Brotherhood Donjon and Kirque and prayerhouse, where proclaimers would rant every Firstday.

Peli examined the sunset critically. The fussy second storey window, with its many tiny panes of thick glass, was wide open; this window at least had hinges!

'Must be a ton of dust up there,' she said.

'Dust?' Yaleen looked up from her packing, which was almost done.

'Why, to make such sunsets as we've seen! It isn't at all cloudy. So the reason must be dust.'

Yaleen joined her friend at the window. True enough, only the faintest muslin brushstrokes of cloud hung aloft. Yet most of the sky-dome was dyed garishly.

Peli waved a hand westward. 'I'll warrant there's been a huge sandstorm in the desert. What price this madcap scheme of yours if the balloon runs into a sandstorm? That's if it ever gets off the ground!'

'Balloons generally get off the ground, Peli dear.'

'Ah, but will the scheme? What will the river temple say? You need their blessing.'

'Hmm,' said Yaleen. 'We'll see.'

'So what *do* you do, supposing there's a sandstorm?'

'We'll be floating high, Peli. That's where the winds are that'll take us eastward.'

'Eastward forever, never to return.'

'You old doom-monger!' Yaleen ran a fingertip along the windowsill, held it up stained grey. 'It's just ordinary dirt,

171

not desert dust.' By way of cleaning her finger she printed the tip on the cracked tawdry plaster of the wall.

'How I hate this dump,' growled Peli. 'Just look at that street down there. Hounds nuzzling turds – human, I'll be bound. And this is the posh part of town. Can't wait to get back to civilization!'

'Bit grimy in Guineamoy, too.'

'That's for a reason – industry! – not from sheer sluttishness. At least in Guineamoy men never look daggers at a girl for going about her own business.'

Yaleen chuckled. 'Should we give the Sons a lesson in spit 'n' polish? Scrub the building from stem to stern? Spend all night at it, leaving it gleaming in the morn? You'll be a boatswain yet, Peli.'

'Not likely. When a permanent mission gets here, *they* can set to with their scrubbing brushes.' She still stared at the sky. 'Superstitious dogs, these Sons! I wonder if they're taking all that blood up there as an omen? Started when we arrived here, fortnight ago; been the same ever since. Let's hope our team have been able to scare them with the skyblaze. Or the Sons might just think it's a sign to take knives to our throats on the way home.'

'Hey, you're kidding.'

'I dunno. We aren't in on the negotiations.'

'Oh come on: Tamath and Marti have told us a fair bit.'

'Yes, to wise us up to the local taboos. I do hope our bosses aren't contemplating *us* as future embassy cooks and bottle-washers.'

'They'd better not be. I have my own plans.'

'Of sailing upon a sandstorm; don't I know it. Let's hope the local shitheads see all that red stuff as the blood of birth.' And Peli mimicked Tamath's stance and style. 'The birth of a new and productive relationship between our two great riverbanks, blah blah. Rather than the blood of death. Been enough of that.'

172

'Birthblood? Looks more like a massive haemorrhage to me.'

'So it's a big birth. Of a new way of life: west and east seeing eye to eye, sort of. Them treating their women a bit more decent. Less of them imposing their riverphobia on the ladies. Their women might even take up boating.'

'I don't believe,' said Yaleen suddenly, 'that these sunsets have anything to do with the desert. I think something else shook up all that dust.' She shivered as she spoke. 'I think it was the Pause, Peli.'

Peli was silent for a while. Then she snorted.

'Of course, don't blame the desert for anything!'

'It was the Pause,' Yaleen repeated.

'Just you shut up about that. There was no Pause, or whatever you call it. That's all in your imagination. I don't know what gives you such ideas.'

'You felt it, too – when the whole world paused for a moment. Why not admit it?'

'Okay, maybe there was an earthquake. A little one.'

'Was there? Everyone skipped a heartbeat, all at once? That wasn't any earthquake.'

'Was. It stirred up stacks of dust out in the desert; because that's where it happened. What do you know about earthquakes? They don't happen once in a blue sun. Stands to reason, everyone's heart would skip a beat.'

'The sun *is* blue, Peli.'

'Clever you. You won't fluster me that way. "Once in a blue sun" is just a word-fossil. Obviously we all once hailed from a world where the sun wasn't even a bit blue.'

Yaleen inspected her fingerprint upon the wall. 'Something else happened. I'm sure!'

'Didn't.'

'Oh have it your own way. At least you'll agree we don't have to bother about sandstorms.'

'We? Who's *we*?'

173

'Tam. Hasso. Me. Anyone else who's coming with us.'

'Tam and Hasso, indeed! You'll have your work cut out.'

'I can balance them. I can handle it.'

'Now get this straight: *I'm* not coming along. Specially not to occupy Hasso while you're busy with Tam, and vice versa. That's why you really want me along, isn't it? Come on, confess.'

'Oh, you.'

'Hey, here come our diplomats.' Peli hauled the window shut.

The sun had sunk by now. The blood was draining from the sky. From the Kirque a bell tolled lugubriously; and it occurred to Yaleen that during that strange moment a fortnight ago the whole world had seemed to ring like a bell. She fingered up more dust from the inside sill and placed the tip of her finger back upon the print on the plaster. When she took her hand away she could detect no smudging, no overlapping of the intricate whorls of skin-lines. She'd achieved a perfect fit. For some reason she found the lack of change in the print both gratifying and alarming.

'What are you playing at now?' said Peli. 'They'll be famished and parched!'

As indeed they were. They, being senior Guildmistress Marti, her junior Tamath, Truthseeker Stamno, and Captain Martan of the 'jack army. The four 'jack soldiers who acted as escort and porters (and perhaps as a covert jungleguild caucus?) took themselves off to their own quarters.

In the dining room, Peli poured local mild ale for the diplomats while Yaleen unwrapped the buffet dinner of cold mutton and pickles.

'Do join us,' invited Marti.

174

'Honoured, I'm sure,' said Peli. 'Thanks, 'Mistress.' She poured ale for herself and Yaleen, but ignored plates; the two of them had eaten earlier.

'Though first, you might light something.'

The dining room, with its stained saggy ceiling, its great creaky floorboards which old varnish and the dirt of years conspired to blacken, and its single window which didn't open, was growing gloomier by the moment. This was a lunky old house which the western Brotherhood had assigned to the mission from the recently victorious east; though at least it was close to the other governmental edifices, and spacious. Maybe for Manhome South it was the height of elegance. Peli hastened to flame an oil lamp.

'Reason why I asked you to stop,' said Marti a while later, as she battled a slice of boiled sheep, 'is that a couple of Sons are joining us after dinner. This pair'll be sent as ambassadors to us, so I want as many eyes as possible to look them over. They aren't true bigwigs yet, but they *were* close associates of a certain Doctor Edrick who died in the war. He was one of the biggest wigs of all.'

'Do the most important Sons really wear wigs when they're in council?' asked Yaleen.

Marti smiled. 'Of course. That's to hide the horns on their heads.'

Peli cleared her throat circumspectly. 'But 'Mistress, I thought the idea was for them to send women representatives? You know, to improve the status and dignity of women over here?'

Tamath laughed sourly. 'Oh yes. We wanted their best women sent. There's a remarkable lack of candidates.'

'Are the Sons putting obstacles in the way?'

'Not exactly, Peli,' said Marti. 'There just *aren't* any best women – as yet. I'm sure there will be, after a few years of witnessing our embassy at work in Manhome. Things will change. But not overnight! Meanwhile, these two particular

175

Sons seem the best of a bad bunch. At least they're comparatively sympathetic. And they're bright; more flexible than the prime bigwigs. We need to know this pair, um, informally. Maybe get them drunk. That's why I asked you to stay, Peli.'

'Oh thank you, 'Mistress. Glad to hear that this old tosspot has her uses.'

Marti laughed. 'Okay, unfortunately phrased!' Noticing Yaleen staring at her, she added, 'Oh yes, and you too, Yaleen. You're only a *gairl*, as they say over here. But you've won your ticket. You risked death by stingers to save Marcialla from drowning, that time she fell from the main yard; didn't you? You're already a good boatwoman, if wayward and flighty. You're proof of our way of life. So if those two Sons have a few drinks with us, they'll see – '

'How I can hold my tipple?'

The guildmistress sighed. 'I was going to say, that we can all relax on equal terms.'

'Pardon me, 'Mistress,' said the 'jack Captain, Martan, 'I'm not planning to relax too much. I want to winkle out of these two fellows how they're set up regarding the fungus drug. We never got very satisfactory answers to that, did we?'

'While for my part,' declared Stamno, that unprepossessing Truthseeker with the mincing turn of phrase, 'I should dearly like to explore the possible relationship between *their* drug, which suppresses riverphobia – and *our* drug, which allows us to glimpse the ineffable. Thus, to pierce those veils of obfuscation with which the world, and the people in it, wrap themselves!'

Peli hoisted an eyebrow. 'He's obfusced me, all right,' she murmured at Yaleen.

'You be a good Seeker and don't get too soaked,' said Tamath. 'See if you can detect when they're telling the truth.'

'I should *never* contemplate blunting my faculties with excess alcohol!'

'Jolly party this'll be,' remarked Peli to no one in particular.

'Oh I'll certainly make a show of drinking,' Martan said. He turned to Stamno. 'Tamath's just teasing you. Let's you and me try to find why they really ran out of their new drug, hmm?'

'And whether we can ever produce it for ourselves! And control the supply!' Yaleen exclaimed, though no one had asked her opinion.

Yaleen's intervention provoked a furious scowl from Tamath. Martan, on the other hand, looked thoughtful. Marti adopted an expression of nonchalant disinterest.

'Aha.' Stamno's eyes crossed – this was one of his less endearing traits – as he focused upon the hidden truth of this moment. 'Do I detect a naïve young person happening to pierce one of those very veils to which I have just alluded? Let me see . . . We men, whether of west or of east, are all inhibited – are we not? The western Sons feel a huge instinctive revulsion against the river and its mighty flow. Whereas we in the east can sail the river once in our lives, and only once, to get wed. Now along comes a certain drug, discovered here in the west, whereby the western soldiery can overcome their inhibition temporarily – '

'We know all that.' Tamath tried to shut him up.

'So they invade the east. Yet subsequently their supply of anti-inhibitor drug dries up. Consequently they can't reinforce – and we win the war. In so doing we capture a small remaining stock of the drug, courtesy of which I am here today together with my good colleague Captain Martan.

'How do our 'pothecaries fare in their analysis of this drug? Not well, I hear. And maybe it is all for the best that they fare poorly? Maybe success on their part would turn our society topsy-turvy! And maybe, too, control of the *source* of the drug – namely the fungus, supposing that it grows in our own jungles – will set the political pattern of the future.

'This pattern might be envisaged in one style by the river guild – but in quite another style by our other guilds! From the point of view of the river guild the ideal situation might well be a useful *trickle* of the drug, but not a flood. Is it then coincidence that our two impending guests – those whom the guild prefers as ambassadors – are also reputedly the original discoverers of the fungus drug?'

'Reef your sails!' snapped Tamath. 'You're racing head-long into Precipices.'

'Oh gosh,' said Yaleen, dismayed at what her guileless contribution had provoked.

Stamno swung round. He trapped her in his cross-eyed stare. His eyes focused on a point just before his own nose, in such a way that his gaze seemed to divide, bend around, and drill a hole through the back of Yaleen's skull.

Stamno mightn't booze, but suddenly he was intoxicated – with himself. 'I perceive a thin black barrier hundreds of leagues long running down the whole midstream of our river! This barrier is one which only *men* heed; and then, not with their eyes. It is inscribed only in the brain. For men to dare this barrier, is to risk madness, sickness, and death. Who inscribed it, but our distant ancestors? Those who were ancestors of our ancestors? Yet a drug erases its black ink for a while. What is written, can be unwritten. Then written again otherwise!'

'Control yourself!' Marti pitched her voice like a slap on the cheek. 'Our guests will be here soon. You're babbling balderdash.'

'Quite,' said Martan. Martan was a practical man, to whom a tree was a tree. Far from stimulating his train of thought, Stamno's outburst had knocked it on the head.

Repelled, he drew his chair noticeably away from the Truthseeker. Stamno refocused, and looked crestfallen.

A moment later the door-gong boomed.

The names of the two Sons were Jothan and Andri. Jothan was a red-head; Andri's hair was jet black. Both men wore beards which had recently seen scissor-work. Their drink was strong ale. Therefore jugs of this were poured, and replenished, and no one retired till nearly midnight.

Later, as Yaleen was about to bed down with a whirlpooling head, she recalled a sozzled Captain Martan blinking at her in a puzzled way at one stage, and muttering, 'I shouldn't be here. Shouldn't at all. Dear me, what am I saying? I've no idea!' He covered his flagon with his palm. 'Enough. Obviously I've had enough. Damn this ale. What *am* I doing here?'

'Mistress Marti patted his arm. 'Whenever we're feeling confused, Captain, we should be guided by tradition.'

'Exactly!' said he. 'Exactly. But our guests are guided by their own traditions. That's the whole bother of it.'

The Son called Andri grinned like a hound about to bite. 'We're all of us guided by the words of life; that's a fact. What guides us is words a million million letters long, written in our flesh. *Our* words here in the west are spelt a bit different from yourn in the east. And our words say "no" to the river, while our women's words say summat contrary. Your men's words say "no – except once"; and your women's words say the same as our women's. Who's to say which spelling is the right 'un? Happen yourn's a prettier way to spell. Happen indeed.' Andri regarded Yaleen across the table for rather too long a time, till with a creepy feeling Yaleen thought that the man fancied himself as owning her, using her for his amusement.

'You'll benefit by a spell in the east,' she said to him. 'Men know how to behave like human beings there.'

'I never had no truck with incinerating women, let me tell you! And we've stopped that now. Part of our peace agreement, right? Now we'll receive fine wines and gems and oh, all sorts.'

'The goods we'll trade aren't bribes to ensure good conduct, sir!' said Marti.

'Didn't say as they was. Though happen we'll pay for 'em sometimes in conduct rather than coin.' Dismissing Marti from his attention, Andri returned his gaze to Yaleen.

Marti would not be so easily dismissed. 'Plus a decent road to the riverside, sir, built by you. And a proper quayside there, with your women in charge of it.'

'Yes, yes.' Andri continued his scrutiny of Yaleen. 'Have you thought,' he said to her, 'you so slim and fresh, with the nutbrown hair and that beautyspot on your neck all unveiled! – have you thought that mayhap the agency as wrote those words in our flesh intended all of us to act humanely, by *limiting* what us men can do? 'Cause we're descended from beasts with a taste for territory and flesh, and a yearning to shove our squirter into any woman as looks good; and when our dander rises we snarl and hack and rampage.

'Only, that agency limited us wrong – by making us men madly fear big stretches of water. We said a flat no to the river – and to our women, too, who like the waves. We didn't let women take the lead, as you did. We specialized ourselves, like piranha-mice as can only ravage whatever's in their way; then fall asleep oblivious. Truesoil, I'm saying now, sweet maid.' He leered.

Eat dirt, thought Yaleen. But she buttoned her lip.

'In my opinion,' said Marti, 'our origins must needs remain a mystery – at least till such time in the far future when perhaps we can sail the sky, and find out. Right now, the shape of that future's up to us. We shall change what was written in the past. Bit by bit.'

'Change what was written!' echoed Martan drunkenly. He hadn't done too well at only making a show of drinking.

Andri gazed at Marti. 'Happen a person *can* wash out the dye he's first dipped in. Or leastways change the hue. Happen I need one of your fine gentle ladies to rub myself up against, to teach me graces? Get to know her really well.' He took a swig of ale then tilted his flagon in Yaleen's direction. 'As a human being.'

Yaleen decided it was high time to knock her own ale-pot over. Or maybe the pot knocked itself over; she wasn't sure.

'Oops!'

Yaleen dreamt a peculiar dream. For as long as the dream endured – and who can say how long that is? – she was convinced that she was wide awake; until some backyard cockerel crowed, and the dream fled from her awareness . . .

She was standing in the Kirque of Manhome South, a building she had never been inside. Even so, she knew that it was the Kirque.

The interior was blue and cavernous. Ribbed and buttressed walls curved upward to a vaulted roof. The floor was of bumpy turquoise cobbles, which felt strangely soft underfoot. Mauve-fronded ferns sprayed out from terracotta pots; the air smelled of dead fish.

In the midst of the Kirque stood a hillock of white marble, with steps mounting one side. Chiselled into the front of the hillock was a word, *Ka-theodral*, which meant nothing to her. From the apex rose a tall marble reading-stand carved in the shape of a flutterbye. The open wings held a heavy volume.

A man popped up behind the reading-stand. He was nude and totally bald of any hair. His whole body was as blanched and soft and sickly-looking as a war casualty's whose bandages have just been taken off. His flesh was poached egg-white. He looked like a giant jungle-grub. Yet from the man's cross-eyed expression Yaleen knew that he must be Truthseeker Stamno.

Gripping the open book, Stamno proclaimed at her:

'What you write, so let it be! But do you remember when the void bubbled up about you in the never-ever? You might have dived into a private time and place. Into a personal universe! Thus everything happening to you thereafter – '

'Voids?' cried Yaleen. 'Bubbles? What are you talking about?'

'I don't say that you *did* do so. I only say that you may have done. Alternatively, when you died into the *Ka*-store – '

'The what?'

' – of the Worm – '

'*Who*?'

' – when you died with your mind split in madness, then also you might have woven a world-for-one. Or on the other hand the Worm might have woven it for you.'

'I don't understand a word of this! Shut up!'

'Then again, maybe we should consider the effects of the timestop drug? Unusual effects, in your case. Exceptional effects. While time halted, during the Pause a whole skein of private events might unwind.'

'Pause? What do you know about the Pause?'

'I don't say that such suppositions are true. Merely, that they might be true.'

'Who are you?'

The grub-man gurgled out a laugh. 'Who am I, indeed? A Seeker of Truth? A ghost of a Worm? The voice of the void? Or of the assembly of the dead? Or of all the worlds which might have been?' The naked man stabbed an accusing finger at her. 'Or am I simply *you* Yaleen? Maybe everyone is you!'

Although Yaleen didn't understand this, she felt terrified. She fled from the Kirque out into the open air.

Where a cockerel crowed.

Whereupon she awoke.

And awaking, forgot.

As she lay abed, calmed by dawn light, listening to the doodle-do of the bird and the soft snores issuing from Peli in the neighbouring bed, to her astonishment Yaleen discovered that she was wearing a ring. A diamond ring! Scrambling from the covers, she darted to the window, the better to examine her discovery.

The ring must have cost upward of sixty fish!

She had never owned a ring before. Yet for some odd reason this particular ring seemed to belong on her finger – as though it had always been there, but invisibly and intangibly.

Quickly she roused her friend.

'Oh thank you, Peli dear! It's lovely. It's too much. What a surprise.'

'Eh? Uh? What?' Peli struggled blearily to focus on the hand held before her face.

'Does this mean that you'll come along in the balloon, Peli? Does it? Or, oh dear, is it your way of saying sorry, no, adieu?'

'What you talking 'bout?'

'This! Your gift. The ring you slipped on my finger while I was zonked out!'

Abruptly Peli sat up. 'I did *not*. No such thing!' She seized Yaleen's hand. 'You're joking. Where did you get that?'

'Do you swear by the river you didn't put this on my finger?'

'Honest. May I puke if I lie.'

183

'But if *you* didn't . . .' Yaleen's hand leapt to her mouth. 'That man Andri! He was giving me the eye last night.'

'An eye's one thing; a diamond ring's another.'

'He must have come back in the wee hours! *They* chose the house for us – maybe there's a tunnel from outside leading to the cellar. He must have crept up here and done this without waking me.'

'How romantic.'

'I don't think it's romantic. He's put his mark on me, Peli, like a farmer tagging a cow. Probably thinks he owns me now. Or that I owe him something. Or whatever rogue thoughts infest their heads over here. I'm going to throw this away. I reject it. I'll leave it on the pillow.'

'Don't be daft, a lovely ring like that.'

Yaleen tugged tentatively at her finger. On second thoughts she settled the ring back. 'I, um, I don't want to take it off.'

'Don't! Wear it. Enjoy it. We'll be shot of this dump before you can say hickity-pickity. Why not write a rude message to him on the window pane? Then if he comes snooping once we're gone . . . No, better not. He's s'posed to be one of the decent Sons, eh? I still can't credit he sneaked in here. But the nerve of it, if he did!' Peli inspected her own hands. Comically downcast, she said, 'Don't I rate a ring, too?'

'You can have it, Peli! Take it. I mean that, honest. I'll likely just lose it, up in one of your sandstorms in the sky.'

'Don't be silly. It's yours. And my fingers are all too big. Tell you what: scratch your name on the window with it. That'll mean it's yours for ever and ever.'

'Okay. I will, too.'

So therefore, in spidery style, Yaleen cut her name upon one of the crude little greenish panes. Close up, the glass distorted the view of the Kirque beyond. Each tiny motion

184

of her head, as she worked, either compressed or stretched the building.

'Vandalizing embassies, eh!' Peli chortled. 'What'll it come to next?'

'Huh. Small beer, this, compared with how they vandalized Verrino.'

'That's all water down the river now. But their beer isn't water. Nor all that small! Oof, my head. What a way to wake up.'

Yaleen stepped back to admire her efforts. The pane looked as if it had been signed by a shaking, arthritic grandmother.

A few hours after that, the party of ten easterners departed on their return trek towards the river, where a vessel stood at anchor waiting to convey them back to Guineamoy.

No one waylaid them en route, to try to murder them; so the mission must definitely be accounted a success.

Whilst tramping along, Yaleen started rehearsing excuses just in case the river guild asked her to return to Manhome South as part of the permanent embassy. Or in case they wished her to tarry in Guineamoy, there to receive the embassy from the west, help Andri feel at home, and gentle him. *Her* personal sights were set on the sky, on the desert, and on what lay beyond. Maybe she would be obliged to sign off the river entirely, instead of just taking leave?

On the other hand, the river temple still needed to give its blessing to the proposed expedition. Lacking that, the balloon venture would be taboo.

If the worst comes to the worst, thought Yaleen, *maybe I can live with a taboo? Supposing that Tam and Hasso and their sponsors can.*

Next, she thought to herself: *Is that the real reason why they invited me along? Not because they really love me – but*

185

*because I'm of the river, a member of its guild? Thus they
propitiate the river temple?*

No! They do love me.

*And I love them. I love Tam. Hasso. Tam. One of them; I
don't know which. I'm sure I do.*

*Trouble is, I don't know what it is to be in love! That's
because I've never been in love before.*

But I shall *be in love. That's a promise.*

*What is this thing called love? Maybe I'm in love already?
Without realizing?*

In love with Tam.

Yes, with Tam. Him.

While the *Blue Guitar* sailed away from the western
shore, Yaleen concentrated upon this concept of love –
realizing that by so doing she would indeed truly fall in
love, presently.

Was that the real purpose of this ring she wore? So that
she could present her ring as a love-pledge to Tam?

Hardly! Tam's fingers were so big and knobbly (though
not clumsy, not in the least). In which case, was the ring
mocking her?

Absolutely not. The diamond was brightness, light,
purity of purpose, truth. It sparkled, like sunlight on the
wave tops where the water was chopped by the passage of
the *Blue Guitar*.

The initiative for the balloon expedition had originally
come from Hasso, one of those Observers who spied on the
west bank by telescope from Verrino Spire. Much good
their vigilance had done Verrino town when the western
soldiery invaded, drugged to resist riverphobia! But at least
the Spire had held out; though now that the war was over
and the west bank was less of a mystery, the Observers'
role might have fallen into abeyance – were there not still
outstanding the even greater mystery of what lay beyond

the inland desert, which had swallowed several parties of explorers in the past.

What better way to observe vast new vistas than from the newly invented balloons which Guineamoy's artisans had crafted under the stimulus of war?

But of course this mode of transport was still in its infancy. Whether it would remain just a novelty or would develop into something grander and life-changing depended largely on the say-so of the river guild and river temples. In Manhome South, Guildmistress Marti had stated, 'Whenever we feel confused, we should be guided by tradition.' Even Yaleen allowed that this was a sensible axiom. When it came to the possibilities raised by balloon flight, many factors were involved.

Rampant balloons might upset the traditional female monopoly over trade and communications. They might weaken, or wipe out, the taboo against men travelling more than once, a taboo which for the most part had served eastern society well. The taboo was backed by sound medical sense, since a mental and bodily crisis afflicted any man who broke the prohibition against repeated river travel, and could easily kill him. But if men were able to float high above the river, and so become mobile and taboo-free (disregarding for the moment the problem of the anti-inhibitor drug), men might conceivably try to dominate affairs, as a cockerel treads its hens – something which the Sons in the west had so signally shown might happen. The Sons had turned their own more stringent river-taboo on its head, and forbidden their women to go near the water at all, fighting liquid with fire. Such men in power had proved themselves oppressive, thrusting, warlike.

Westerners needed to mend their ways and learn the womanly, flowing touch. Their own women, emerging from the dark cloud of ignorant centuries, must learn the way to show them; and learn how to sail the river. Yet would that happen, if balloons could carry men hither and thither untrammelled?

Thus balloon travel should only be introduced cautiously, in tandem with social improvements in the west; many 'mistresses said so. Any balloon must be strictly licensed and approved. Otherwise the world might plunge into another such calamity as the Sons' discovery of the fungus 'anti-inhibitor' had unleashed. (It was fortunate that the Sons had so ignorantly exploited the fungus, virtually wiping it out in its jungle haunts! Or so they claimed; a claim lent credence by the abrupt collapse of their war effort.)

On the other hand, the jungle guild were rooting for balloons. Ridiculous to conceive of ever shifting timber by balloon, needless to say! But it was the men of the jungle guild who had made the long march from Jangali to Verrino to win the war. They deserved some recompense for all their suffering and sacrifice; such as a guarantee that *next time* – though pray river there wasn't a next time! – they should fly to war, not walk. So when the trans-desert balloon expedition was mooted by the Observers, the 'jacks supported this. Support also came from certain important industrialists of Guineamoy, purveyors of the weapons used in the war, who saw balloons as a future source of profit.

The prevailing winds mainly blew north or south along the river. However, the weather patterns of the highfleece clouds showed that further up in the atmosphere, and in particular over the area where the desert pressed closest to the river, in the Gangee-Pecawar region, air-streams often blew due eastward. Hence the site selected for assembly and launching: namely Pecawar. To begin with the balloon would drift south as it arose, but then it would enter the east-bound sky-stream. (A hundred leagues further south, high winds often blew in from across the desert towards the west; so there was a fair chance of returning, depending upon the kind of country encountered beyond the eastern desert. Assuming that the desert eventually gave way to hospitable terrain.)

'Let them go!' argued some voices in the river guild. 'Let them equip! Let them launch their balloon! They'll never come back from beyond the desert. Probably there's just desert, and nothing else beyond it. We'll lose our adventurers – bravely, tragically, and foolishly. Balloons will dip in esteem.'

Work on the big balloon began, and continued, but the river temple had still not pronounced the final word of consent. Yet privately guild and temple were sure of one item. If the balloon *were* to fly, young Yaleen of Pecawar should be part of the crew. Her wayward wish should certainly receive the blessing of her guild.

Yaleen herself was determined to be part of the expedition – even if she was compelled to take 'drench leave' as she said fancifully of anyone quitting a boat in mid-passage (to fall foul, no doubt, of stingers). Her friend, Observer Hasso, had promised her. So also had her other friend, Tam the Potter. Tam had used up his one-go on the river to sail to Pecawar to experiment with the unique clays found locally (as well, perhaps, as making a romantic, quixotic gesture in pursuit of Yaleen). On the boat ex Verrino he had fallen in with Hasso, and these two men were soon as close as two slices of bread, glued together by the butter of Yaleen; perhaps foolishly so, should the butter melt one way or the other.

What Yaleen did not know was that though her guild might well favour her dreams of desert flight – even to the extent of publicly nominating her – this was because she was totally dispensable. In fact, therein lay her value. Already her brief career had been marked by various embarrassing scrapes; such as the time when she made a fool of herself at the Junglejack Festival – or that other occasion at Port Firsthome when she teamed up with a party of treasure hunters who were convinced that something rich and rare lay buried under the Obelisk of the Ship, and by burrowing almost toppled the Obelisk. True, she was bold and energetic and even diligent, but such incidents practically guaranteed that at some stage – either literally or metaphorically – she would poke a hole in the balloon. If the guild's rumour-mongers reported accurately, Yaleen bid fair to set two of the expedition men at jealous loggerheads.

This was why the guild had despatched Yaleen on the brief preliminary mission to Manhome South as a jill-of-all and general bottlewasher. Fingers crossed, she was unlikely to provoke any serious contretemps. She went along in a strictly minor capacity – to a place where mere 'gairls' were held in contempt. (And if she did get into hot water, well, she was an example of an independently minded female.) By sending her, the guild promoted her to sufficient prominence to be worth nominating, and subsequently losing . . .

A few days after the *Blue Guitar* docked in grimy Guineamoy, Yaleen was summoned to the river temple. By this time the leaders of the mission had had opportunity to debate their findings in conclave. Yaleen reported to the temple, ready to spill out her excuses. She felt somewhat cocky; somewhat apprehensive.

Her cockiness proceeded simply from the fine diamond she wore. Quite why this should be, she wasn't sure. The ring had rapidly come to seem like a personal talisman. Spirited on to her finger by a lecherous Son, that lucky find had now become her luck; and why not?

Her apprehension came from a different quarter. The very same day that the *Blue Guitar* arrived, Yaleen had been interviewed by a man from the local newssheet, the *Guineamoy Gazette*.

This interview was arranged through the quaymistress's good offices; and it took place in a back room of her office, though the quaymistress showed no desire to eavesdrop or supervise. The newsman was seeking what he called a 'human interest angle' on the trip to the Sons' southerly stronghold.

'I'm hoping this story will be syndicated up and down the river,' the fellow confided to Yaleen. His name was Mulge; but that was his misfortune. The name matched him, though.

He was a grey, stout young man. Grey of skin, as though the sun had never shone on him. Grey of demeanour: stolid, serious, lack-lustre, untouched by much imagination. Pencil-grey, smoke-grey.

'You'll be famous,' he said in a flat tone of voice, as though the notion of such exposure worried him, though equally it was his stock in trade.

Duly, the very next day the following column had appeared in the *Guineamoy Gazette*; and perhaps this ought to be quoted, rather than a blow by blow reprise of the interview itself, since the following is what emerged for public scrutiny and is what was uppermost in Yaleen's mind when she paid her visit to the temple.

Her attempts to enthuse Mulge on the subject of the desert expedition had, it transpired, been so much water off a duck's back. Maybe he thought she was indulging in a different sort of flight – one of fancy. Maybe he wrote to the limits of his understanding – maliciously, so it seemed to Yaleen when she first scanned his column. How he had garbled and idiotized everything. His account read as though he hadn't harked at all. Mulge could as easily have stayed at home and made the whole thing up.

GANGEE 'GAIRL' IN SONS' LAIR

Crewwoman Yaleen of the *Blue Guitar* said yesterday how glad she is to be back in civilization after acting as 'cabin girl' for the momentous peace mission to Manhome South.

'I felt scared all the time,' she confessed. 'But I didn't show it. Those Sons call all young women "gairls", with a sneer in their voice, as if we're kids. But now because of us they've stopped burning women. One of the Sons even fancied me! I didn't fancy him.

'But yes, I'd go back again – into the wild dogs' liar – to show what we're made of over here.'

(This was the bit which worried Yaleen most of all.)

Of her ordeal, Yaleen said . . .

There was more, in similar vein; and the piece ended off thus:

Yaleen's deputy mission commander, Tamath, commented: 'Yaleen's too modest. She behaved as a fine representative of our way of life. She's young but she already distinguished herself on several occasions. She's our finest.'

True, typeface and layout were excellent – though 'lair' was misspelled as 'liar', which seemed appropriate – but on the whole Yaleen had felt like curling up in a dark corner. Alternatively: like coming out with fists flailing.

And why had Tamath said those things? Simply to counteract the impression of breathless naïvety conveyed by the rest of the piece?

Mixed in with her cocktail of embarrassment and defiance, Yaleen also detected a third, odd flavour. This was the sense that, with her interview in print, somehow she was 'emerging' – from anonymous obscurity back into the light, not unlike some death-box buried in Pecawar cemetery being disinterred by the breezes of time.

What became of death-boxes when *that* occurred? Why, they were soon burnt up and destroyed!

Yet Yaleen had always been obscure and anonymous; nobody special, save to friends and family and three or four lovers, and herself. Whence came this sense of familiarity at being mentioned in print? Which was this light she was emerging into? She didn't relish the sensation. It felt wrong, even dangerous.

After mulling the matter over for a while, she decided that basically she was a proud creature. Mulge's column constituted a satire on that pride, a caricature.

So as she approached the river temple that morning along Bezma Boulevard, she felt apprehensive. But she also blew on her ring and polished it and felt proud.

The river temple was a sprawling ancient structure constructed of rusty orange ironstone. Recently the stones had been repointed with yellow mortar, but in years past the walls had bent and bellied and been corseted with metal bands and rings, which were now picked out in black paint. The whole edifice resembled a strongchest for storing treasure; a somewhat grimy and eroded one, despite its refurbishments, due to the pollution in the air.

Indeed the temple did contain treasure. It enshrined the spirit of a way of life – along with the political and moral embodiment of that way of life, the river priestess. Additionally the temple cellar guarded the guild treasury (Guineamoy account). While on the ground floor at the rear this particular temple housed the Mint, which stamped and milled all scales and fins and fish for distribution up and down stream.

By tradition a triumvirate supervised the Mint; this trio consisting of a 'mistress of the river guild, plus a Guineamoy metalmaster, plus a 'witness woman' from as far away as possible. Once every two years a new witness was elected, alternately by the towns of Tambimatu and Umdala. For manufacturing reasons the Mint must needs be sited at Guineamoy. For historic reasons the river guild gave it a roof. The witness ensured that new coins all duly entered circulation, and did not slip 'through chinks in the floorboards' down into the river guild treasury in the cellar below.

Yaleen entered by the arched doorway, gave her name to the clerk-acolyte on duty, and was led to priestess Kaski's parlour for her audience.

When she was shown in, the parlour was empty. Cushions lay scattered on the polished hoganny floor before a low throne. A single mullioned window gave sight of the river, where a brig was sailing by. Old tapestries showing ancient boats cloaked the walls.

These tapestries caused Yaleen a momentary sense of terrible unease. Instead of admiring them, she focused her gaze upon the genuine vessel sailing the waters.

A rustle. A swirl of fabric. And Kaski appeared – stepping directly out of one of the tapestries! The tapestry was actually in two separate parts, though they had hung as one. Behind, a door was concealed.

Supporting herself with a silver-tipped cane, Kaski hobbled slowly in the direction of her throne. Yaleen almost darted to assist; but this might have been impertinent. Besides, the shrivelled old woman had paid no heed to her yet. Yaleen shuffled uncertainly.

Then the crone did reach her throne – and swung round, sitting smoothly and swiftly, not at all like somebody suffering from crippled joints. Her eyes took in Yaleen, with piercing familiarity.

'River bless you, child of the flow!' The priestess's voice was clear, purposeful, precise.

Yaleen realized that Kaski must have been watching her

194

for a while through a crack in the divided tapestry before emerging. And that slow walk of hers had been hoo-ha, designed to put Yaleen off stride. Maybe Kaski could fence with that cane of hers in as sprightly a style as any 'jack soldier. Perhaps she could tap-dance rings around Yaleen.

'River lave you, 'Mistress Priestess.'

'Hmm. Read that story about you in the paper, I did!' said Kaski without more ado.

'Oh dear. Honestly, I've never seen such a jumble of drivel in a newssheet – not even at 'Barbra! It makes me out such a silly chit.'

Kaski, however, rapped her cane on the floor. 'Yaleen, you should realize that *all* reports are garbled to a greater or lesser degree. Even the best newssheets are always a sort of fiction concocted out of what's real. This is simply the first time you have encountered the phenomenon from both sides: as reader and as originator of the news.'

'He even got my home-town wrong.'

'Gangee's nearer to here than Pecawar,' said Kaski airily. 'And "Gangee girl" has a better ring to it, wouldn't you say?'

'Nor did I describe myself as a cabin girl!'

'Not to worry. It's the spirit that counts.'

'I certainly didn't say I was panting to go back west.'

'Aha, here we have the nub. You want to go on that mad balloon expedition instead.'

The suspicion dawned on Yaleen that Mulge might have been manipulated by Tamath in what he wrote. How could she avoid going back west, should the guild ask her to – when thousands of people had been informed that Yaleen was their junior champion?

Alternatively: how could she avoid lingering in Guine-amoy to be hospitable to visiting Sons? Thus to make up for her rude remarks about them (which she hadn't uttered quite so)? If *that* was what the guild preferred.

Which way did the rudder point?

'Oh,' she said.

But again old Kaski surprised her. The priestess chuckled. 'Never fear, child! We intend to give our benediction to the balloon scheme. *And*, what's more, to your participation in it. In fact, you will become our official representative. There, how's that?'

What a shift of the wind to an unexpected quarter!

'Eh?' said Yaleen.

'I believe you heard me well enough.'

'Ah. Yes. Um. Can Peli be part of the expedition too?'

Now Kaski frowned. 'What's this? Your friend Peli?'

'She's very competent.'

'I'm aware of it. Is she asking to go?'

'Not *quite*. I could persuade her, with your blessing.'

'You'll do no such thing. It would be wholly unethical to pressure such a competent crew member into quitting the river.'

'Who's quitting? We'll be back.'

'Mind your manners! You presume too much. The guild does not give its blessing to Peli going, especially when she has no wish to do so.' As if to soften the severity of this, Kaski added, 'To be sure, you'll be back . . .'

'My apologies.'

'Accepted. It's good that you've had this exposure in the newssheets.'

'Is it?'

'This establishes you as a personality, expedition-wise. You're up front, as *our* person. I'm sure you won't let us down. Nor for that matter, the balloon.' Wreathed in wrinkled smiles, Kaski arose nimbly from her throne.

Ro-ses are bloo-ming in Pecawar – !

Yaleen whistled this old tune to herself as she trod the

dust of her home town on her way to visit the expedition headquarters.

Capiz Street stretched out eastward towards open country, accompanied by its aqueduct along which a rill of water purled.

At this distance from the riverside and the Wheelhouse, the aqueduct had descended nearly to ground level. Its piers were only three bricks high. Its gutter had narrowed to concentrate what was left of the flow. Entry to the walled gardens of houses on that side of the road was by little bridges which stepped up over the 'duct; whereas closer to the town centre the piers were high enough to walk beneath.

This whole network of 'ducts which carried water to homes and irrigated gardens still enchanted and intrigued Yaleen almost as much as it had when she was a child. Truly, the system was one of the wonders of Pecawar. (The second wonder being the many rose gardens, both public and private, which availed themselves of the moisture.) The flow commenced high and huge at the Wheelhouse by the river. There, giant archimedean screws forever quarried water; themselves powered by great wooden waterwheels which a headrace flume kept in constant motion. The prime source soon branched into a number of different, slowly descending, circuitous aqueducts, which branched and branched in turn – till out by the edge of town where she now walked, a 'duct would be diminuendo, about to peter out.

The elevated 'duct system had been in place a hundred years and more. Its designer of genius, architect Margeegold of Aladalia, had paid close attention to another, and complementary, sort of flow: to wit, the smooth passage of people and goods through the Pecawar streets. Hence the many convolutions of the network, even downtown where the 'ducts marched high. Moving further from the source, the branching 'ducts as they descended often compelled lesser streets to tunnel underneath, or bridge up and over with ramps or flights of steps. In the past this had proved a cause of complaint to the elderly who could remember a flat, no-fuss Pecawar. To Yaleen's way of thinking all these ups and downs brought some of the charm of Verrino to an otherwise level town. Maybe she had even elected to become a riverwoman in the first place thanks to Margee-gold's aqueducts; for riverwater continually bubbled through her home town, along red brick veins, like lifeblood.

Without a map it was hard to say which branches led where. Whether the Pemba Avenue 'duct ultimately watered her home neighbourhood – or the Zanzyba Road one! As a child, oblivious to the likely existence of an official plan (or rather, disdaining this type of adult approach to something enchanting), she and her friends had formed a gang pledged to solve the riddle of the waterways. This, they had set out to achieve by perilously scaling downtown piers and launching paper boats with identification marks on them. Then they had raced off to try to catch these, much further down 'duct. In a papery way she was already becoming a boatwoman.

One day her brother Capsi tried to spoil this fine sport by presenting his own pen and ink diagram of the network – the true layout, so he claimed, arrived at by observation and deduction.

Yaleen and friends had snatched his work. In furious petulance at Capsi's blindness to the unwritten magic rules of their boat-chasing game, they had torn the map up and floated the pieces away.

But thereafter the magic perished. The gang didn't scale any more piers. Besides, they had already been hauled down on two separate occasions and harangued by an aquaguild worker. Capsi, for his part, became alienated after that. He concentrated his attention upon the further shore, which was then still taboo . . .

As Yaleen walked along, whistling repetitively, her mind had wandered back into past. Now the tune suddenly restored her to herself.

Roses were blossoming indeed. Climbers sprawled over garden walls. Here, *Zéphirine Drouhin* the thornless rose bloomed carmine-pink, its rich scent strongly assailing the passer-by. There, *Felicity and Perpetuity* rambled its red-flecked ivory rosettes.

Ahead, a grey globe loomed over walls and rooftops: the 'first stage' of the balloon! It had been just the beginnings of a framework of split bamboo the last time she saw it. Yaleen quickened her step and presently she arrived at the workyard from which balloon and gondola would rise one day soon.

At once she caught sight of Tam and Hasso labouring together on the gondola. *That* hadn't even existed when she sailed from Pecawar. A true boat on the sky, it now rested in a supporting cradle underneath the tethered globe.

Other men were working, too – she recognized Observer Tork, and Farge from Guineamoy – but it was Hasso and Tam for whom she had eyes.

Tam most of all. Tam.

Yes, she *did* love him. She knew that now. She had rehearsed loving him times enough on the voyage back from Guineamoy. In so doing she had found that a person could indeed teach herself to believe in love by concentrating; by invoking the image of that love a sufficient number of times – like a piece of music much practised till playing it became second nature. Oh yes, there was an art to love, akin to complex music. This art was distinct from the skill of sexual pleasure, which was a simpler tune that the body played. Just a tune. Love was (could be, should be) a symphony, a heart-chorale.

And now the actual music-drama of this love could get under way; though Hasso, her other former partner in the tune of sexual amusement, must of course remain a sweet friend.

She broke into a run across the yard. 'Tam! Hasso! Tam!'

The men turned. Hasso started towards her. But Tam stepped past him, for she had called Tam's name twice; and it was into his arms that Yaleen jumped. Tam hugged her, released her. She spun; and touched Hasso's hand, but only touched it.

She laughed. 'I'm back!'

'From the wild dogs' lair, eh?' Hasso gave a wicked grin.

'Oh, *that*! Listen you two: the river temples have given their blessing. And what's more, *I'm* my guild's chosen nominee − to fly! They haven't just said okay; they've made me their official representative.'

'What marvellous news,' said Tam.

Hasso nodded. 'It's all in the latest newssheet, of course.'

'Really? I haven't been home yet. Left my kit in town; rushed straight out here.'

'To your future home-from-home.' Tam stretched his right hand invitingly towards the light wooden gondola. This gesture tugged his sleeve up, exposing the queer thin red birthmark which ran full circle round his wrist.

'Definitely worth a fortnight in Manhome South, to prove your mettle,' said Hasso. 'Seriously, I mean it.'

The two men were competing subtly. But did not Hasso already sound just a tad resigned? Perhaps even cynical, with a hint of bitterness? She certainly hoped not; that would be a shame.

Though if Hasso read the signs aright – of her plunge into Tam's arms – was he not obliged to withdraw somewhat?

Not really!

At this point one of the motives behind her decision to prefer Tam became crystal clear to Yaleen. Maybe it was a kindly motive; maybe it was selfish. The fact was that Hasso was sufficiently experienced in the ways of the world to play second fiddle; whereas Tam could have been deeply, heartachingly hurt.

Damn it, why should there *be* any need for a choice between them?

Ah but there had to be, if she was to explore the full symphony of love, all the obsessive ache of it (as opposed to convivial amorousness).

Tam seized up Yaleen's hand. He held it, stroking her fingers. 'Hey, what's this?'

'Oh, my ring?'

'Noticed it right away,' commented Hasso. 'Ve-ry pretty. Gift from an admirer?'

'You could say so.'

'How's that?' asked Tam, letting go her hand in panic; at which Hasso smiled and looked serene.

'Long story! Tell you all about it later. Look, don't I rate a drink? I'm parched.'

Hasso jerked a thumb at the smaller of the two substantial storage sheds. 'I've a bottle of decent vintage stowed over there.'

'I think I'd prefer ale if there's any.' Yaleen waited a moment before turning to Tam, so as not to seem to snub Hasso.

'I could easily run and fetch a jugful,' Tam offered. 'It isn't far.'

'Shouldn't take him more than half an hour,' said Hasso.

'Oh Tam, you mustn't bother! That's ridiculous. How about coffee? Or lemonade?'

Tam brightened. 'Lemonade, it is!'

So the three friends headed for the shed.

Part of the shed was stacked with dried food, preserves, blankets, empty demijills for water, and such. Yaleen spotted an unmade bed.

'Is one of you sleeping out here?'

'Somebody has to, to guard the balloon and basket,' said Hasso.

'Gondola,' Tam corrected him. 'It's much bigger than a basket.'

'Like a little boat,' agreed Yaleen.

Tam fetched a flagon of lemonade to a table spread with charts. These charts were mainly blank. A couple of Tam's pots with sprays of *Pink Parfait* roses glowing through the glaze weighed them down. Tam poured a couple of glassfuls, glanced at Hasso, poured a third.

'We've decided on a name,' he said.

'A name?'

'For the balloon, of course! Boats have names. A boat of the air deserves one – we're going to call it *Rose*.'

'Because we hope it'll rise,' joked Hasso. 'Myself, I thought we should call it *Dough*. But I got outvoted.'

'Ho ho,' said Tam. 'I'm going to paint a huge pink hybrid tea rose on the globe. *Gavotte* or *Stella*; haven't made my mind up yet.'

Yaleen caressed the flowers painted on one of the pots. '*Rose*: I like it. Good choice. Emblem of Pecawar, eh? I'd have voted that way myself.'

It was more diplomatic, she thought, to describe the rose as symbol of Pecawar rather than as Tam's own adopted motif. He had begun to decorate his pots with roses back in Aladalia soon after he had got to know Yaleen and had first gone to bed with her. Before that, his pots had usually sported fleuradieus in various shades from light blue to dark purple, depending on his mood.

They drank lemonade, they talked. They visited the other shed, where she admired the waxed silken bags of the balloon's 'second stage' folded up neatly in three white mounds.

The balloon needed two stages if it was to rise high enough to catch the easterlies. The globe alone could not do the job. Buoyed up by hot air rising through a chimney from a heater in the gondola, the globe would only hoist its burden eight thousand spans into the sky at most; and that was going at full blast, which would burn up too much oil too soon. To enter the highfleece region required more altitude: twice that height. Thus a cluster of three great gasbags would tower above the globe, quite dwarfing it. These would be inflated with the lightest of all gases, watergas. Supplies of bottled watergas came from Guinea-moy, where it was obtained by destructively distilling coal in closed iron retorts to produce coalgas, from which the fire-damp was later removed. The globe would hoist the gondola. The gasbags in turn would hoist the globe; and the hot air rising up around the globe would magnify the natural lift of the watergas.

What's more, much of the watergas could be pumped back down through condenser valves into the bottles mounted around the crown of the globe. Thus the gasbags would flop sufficiently for the whole ensemble to descend at journey's end without any need to vent and waste the irreplaceable watergas. (Given time, and being so light, watergas could waste itself well enough by breathing out through the skin of the bags.) By this means the balloon ought to be able to ascend a second time, perhaps even a third. By this means they might return home.

It was Tam, with his knowledge of furnaces and clays, who had cooked up the strong lightweight ceramics for use in the hot-air breeder, gas-jars, pumps and such; thus solving a problem which had foxed the factories of Guineamoy with their prejudice in favour of heavy lumps of metal.

Of steering, the balloon had none. As yet, steering – by means of wooden fans turned by compressed air – was inefficient and exacted a toll in added burden. Consequently it had been sacrificed in return for extra altitude and payload. They would sail where the high winds willed, and would hope that they could pace their eventual descent so as to choose a safe, hospitable landing spot. (Still, some time in the future Tam's ceramics would likely lead to the production of powerful lightweight 'engines', which could direct the course of a balloon no matter which quarter the winds blew from.)

Next, they visited the gondola and climbed inside. Tam and Hasso competed in showing her the fittings: canvas hammocks, tiny galley, privy cubicle (with a large hole venting down). Yaleen imagined herself floating through the sky, peeking out of the little window of the privy, and peeing rain – after which a wind wiped her bare bum dry.

Tam displayed the hot-air breeder.

'We *can* convert it to work on charcoal, which we can make out of any wood we find. That won't be as efficient as oil, but it'll still do the job. We'll be glad of the hot air when we're up in the heights of the sky.'

'Why's that? We'll be nearer the sun.'

'Ah, but where do you suppose hailstones drop from? Up there! So the higher you go, the colder it must get.'

She corrected herself: a wind *freezing* her bare bum, while she peed yellow ice.

Hasso explained how partitions and lockers could be dismantled, and reassembled so as to form a big cart – or, depending on terrain, a sledge. After landing they might have to haul the *Rose* some way southward by hand to gain the westerly returning highfleece winds, should the low winds prove unfavourable. The gondola (with its privy stool duly plugged and dogged) would even double as a clumsy boat, using silk for a sail. Should there be water beyond the sands, and the water not provoke a phobia.

For the first time the possibility occurred to Yaleen that they might not be coming back; might not be able to. But she shrugged this prospect off.

After a couple of hours spent at the expedition head-quarters Yaleen departed homeward along Capiz Street with a shopping list in her pocket. Of spices, yet! So that they could pep up their 'wooden rations' and also whatever fodder they found at journey's end, if any. Drench the cooking; kill the taste – said Hasso. She forgave him for his cavalier attitude to meals. He had endured the belt-tightening siege of Verrino Spire, and had learned to despise good food.

Caraway, oregano, chilli powder, pepper, paprika, cloves! She also forgave Hasso for his blithe – and mean – presumption that she had some intimate and cut-price relationship with spice sacks, courtesy of the fact that her dad worked for the industry. Perhaps Hasso just wanted to make her feel, now that the expedition was almost ready, that she was contributing something vital? Well, she was! She was contributing *herself*. She forgave him; but of course when you forgive somebody, that forgiveness comes between you. It separates you by an invisible barrier, where you are the forgiving one, and he is the forgiven; a picture frame, with you as the painter, and him as the painted, coloured a certain hue for ever more . . . or at least for a while.

'Mum! Dad! Is anybody home?'

Yaleen's mother appeared at the head of the stairs. She smiled and held out her arms and descended, her sandals clopping on the waxed treads. She trod the stairs slowly, with a cautious grace.

'Don't hug hard, darling! I'm pregnant.'

'*What?*'

Yaleen's mum laughed. 'You needn't look so surprised. It's possible, you know.'

'Where's Dad?'

'I didn't become pregnant this very moment, daughter dear! Your dad's at work. Where else? I imagine he's busy counting peppercorns.'

'Oh. Of course.' Where *else* would her father be?

Mother appraised her. 'We read of your exploits in the newssheet. And just yesterday we read how you're going to leave us – by balloon. Maybe it's best that we're having another child, your father and I.'

'How do you mean?'

'If your heart's set on this venture I shouldn't try to dissuade you. I imagine that it's a brave thing to do – braver even than going to that vile place in the west. Besides, your guild is honouring you. But who has ever come back from the desert? *Who?*'

'Look, Mum, those earlier expeditions all failed because explorers tried to foot it over the sands. We'll float over fast, and in comfort. It'll be a picnic.'

Besides, thought Yaleen, *I'm in love. At last. Am I not?*

I'm almost in love with love itself! And Tam is my emblem of love; just as surely as love's own emblem is the rose. So obviously I must help him (and the others too; don't forget the others!) to sail our rose of love through the sky to another land, somewhere or wherever.

Then back home again. Back home; goes without saying.

My love is a brave rose balloon. Let nothing blight it. Let no thorn prick it.

Yet why, oh why, should I feel this whelming need to love? This urge to surrender myself – not so much to a particular man (absurd idea!) as to love itself? This need to submerge myself (that's it, submerge!) in an ecstasy of the emotions?

Perhaps a Creator might have felt such an urge, once she had crafted her universe. This desire to submerge Herself in the stream of Being! To surrender Herself to the flow of feeling – so that thus her worlds should be truly alive, free to live as they choose.

(Supposing that there is a Creator! Or ever was. That's an unsatisfactory proposition without much meat on it. A dry bone for Ajelobo savants to chew over.)

Let's look at this another way, hmm? I've spent years crafting my own self. I've crafted my life. Now I must dive into that life headlong – to become who I really am.

Just so, does my mum become a mother again. She does so instinctively, irrationally, capriciously – whatever she says about reasons, after the event! Yet perhaps she does so wisely too, with the wisdom of the heart, not of the head.

Such strange heady thoughts are brewed by love! Such an intoxicating ferment!

All things outside of me – a ring, a rose, a gondola, the sky, those dunes which I have yet to glimpse – all of these connect up with the feelings which are inside me; expressing them, voicing them, illuminating them. That's why love matters: it makes the world bloom with new meaning.

Gently Yaleen embraced her mother. 'Don't worry. I'll be back to play with my new sister!'

'Sister? It might be a brother. Or twins.'

'Oh, I suppose so! Dunno why I said that. You'll come to the launching, won't you, to wave us on our way?'

'I imagine we will.'

'Don't imagine. *Do*!'

Mother laughed. 'Very well!' Only then did she spy the diamond ring on Yaleen's finger. 'That's beautiful. If you fall among savages, you can buy food with it.'

'Maybe we'll fall amongst *aliens*! Among natives of this world who were here before ever our people came. There they'll be on the other side of the sands, hiding in their burrows beneath ruined palaces. Harking to us with their huge ears, or in their dreams.'

'And pigs might fly.'

'If a rose can fly, a pig might fly too.'

'Tonight's won't. We're having fried pork for dinner.'

Dad came home late that evening; though not so late that the pork was spoilt. (Mother had commenced frying, irrespective.) Naturally, Dad was chagrined to be late on this day of days, of his daughter's surprise return. Mother appeared richly amused at his chagrin – though she was amused in a composed, controlled, almost artificial way which struck Yaleen as most peculiar. Mum obviously *relished* something, yet she wasn't going to split her sides laughing. In case she split the sprig of baby loose inside her? Yaleen was quite puzzled.

The truth came out over dinner.

Dad had just dished out an extra dollop of nutmeggy apple sauce on to Yaleen's plate, and he was quizzing her as to whether those Sons used spices much at Manhome South; and if so, what kinds, and how (which in itself was odd, since Dad had never been one to bring work home with him, save for the tang of it on his clothes); when Mum remarked casually, 'By the way, your father's having a love affair.'

'*What*?' Yaleen was flabbergasted. First a baby; now an affair? Had she heard aright? Had Mum really meant what she seemed to mean?

'We're also having a baby, your mother and I,' said Dad. He didn't sound too discomposed, though perhaps he laid undue stress on the 'we'.

'I know you are. Mum said.'

Mum smiled. 'Quite ingenious of your dad, I'd say. He can have an affair *and* a baby. An affair with one woman, a baby with another.' She didn't sound sarcastic; but maybe she was playing a deeper game than simple sarcasm. 'Usually it's the other way about, isn't it? You should know that, Yaleen. A riverwoman has her affairs – and her husband stays home with baby. How the world's changing since the war! All that marching by, and the distant clash of weapons, must have fired ambitions in your dad.'

'Oh.' Yaleen examined the grain of the wood in the kitchen table – a black knot seemed to be coming loose.

'How was she this evening, then?' enquired Mum.

'Fine, thanks. Fine,' said Dad.

'I'm glad to hear it. I'd say we owe her a debt of gratitude. Perhaps we should even ask her to be guidemother to our baby when it's born! You'd imagine that a love affair would, well, dilute the passion of the loins. Divert the seed; water it down. But no. Provenly not.' Mum patted her tummy. 'A lover has to make bigger, fiercer efforts; and this spills over, doesn't it? The lover has to prove how he's big enough for two women. And prove it he does.'

Dad grinned lopsidedly. 'I certainly seem to have done.'

They didn't *seem* to mind discussing this business; though for sure a strand of tension twanged beneath the amiable veneer.

'Do describe your friend, hmm? Tell Yaleen what she looks like.'

'Oh, who cares what she looks like?' said Dad, sounding ever so reasonable. 'Looks, indeed! It's her person that's important. It's what she is, that counts.'

'To be sure! And she's strong. Independent. Assertive. And subtle; but then all women are subtle.'

'Er, what's her name?' Yaleen asked cautiously.

'Her name's Chanoose,' replied Mum. 'She's the quaymistress.'

'Her!'

'Oh yes, I was forgetting you must know her.'

'Well, not intimately.'

'Unlike your father. And despite her strength and independence, this same Chanoose has fallen under your father's spell – as if enchanted. It quite makes me proud.'

Yaleen turned to her dad. 'Was that why you were asking me about the spice-trading prospects over in the west?'

'I don't follow.'

'Has your Chanoose set her eye on exporting best Pecawar spices to the west bank? Those Sons don't need hotting up, you know. They need cooling down. They need blanding, not peppering.'

'No, no, I just asked out of curiosity.'

And so the meal continued, in amiable enough vein, with bluepears in syrup for afters followed by cups of cinnamon coffee.

Later on, when she was in her room, Yaleen tried to assess more calmly her mother's attitude to the recently conceived foetus. Of whose love was it really the product? Why, of Mum's and Dad's, obviously! But wasn't the enigmatic Chanoose in a sense the mother too, even though she didn't bear the child? Didn't Chanoose provide the *catalyst*, as they said of chemicals in Guineamoy? Barren herself, presumably 'safe' from conception, hadn't she nevertheless caused the event to occur? So had Dad given Mum the baby to prove his continuing fidelity, despite the affair? Had Mum insisted upon this, as her price for condoning it? Or had the affair itself transformed Dad in his middle years, compelling him to create new life like a fountain bursting forth in a desert?

And how had he captivated and besotted Chanoose, who had always seemed – from a distance – so aloof and powerful? How had the 'mistress become a mistress, in this strange triple relationship?

Yaleen found herself feeling deeply glad and thankful on her dad's behalf. But what preoccupied her most was the queer way that this affair of her dad's, coupled with his role as sire of a new baby, seemed to reflect her own love-dilemma. What a peculiar model of her own experience! Might she also manage to maintain a similar balance – between herself and Hasso and Tam? Could she? Ought she to try?

Somehow she suspected that the situation involving Mum and Dad and Chanoose was inherently unstable. It was indeed unlike the rompings of a riverwoman in a distant port, reaping wild oats far from her shore-husband's ken. Yet with taboos perhaps about to fray under the pressure of a certain fungus-drug and cross-river intercourse – and with balloons in the offing – might not everyone's current way of life become unstable presently? Might not drug chemistry and balloon technology cause changes which the war itself had failed to cause (though the war might have been the initial catalyst)?

Maybe, maybe not. The river guild and river temples were subtle, old, and unlikely to spring leaks too large to caulk.

She considered recent events again: the mooting of the desert expedition, preparations for this, Chanoose's affair with her father, the pregnancy, her own mission ex Pecawar to Guineamoy thence to Manhome South culminating in her official secondment as guild representative aboard the *Rose*.

Wasn't there something odd about the sequence? Something more than coincidental? Chanoose must have become intimate with her dad at about the time the guild must have seriously started to consider the advantages, and the possible threat, posed by the expedition . . .

No, no, this was nonsense. The day had been long. Yaleen was tired out – by delight at the balloon; by the energy she had poured into her love for Tam, and into the *decision* to prefer him; and finally by her astonishment at her parents' capers.

Chanoose had fallen in love irrationally. 'Enchanted' had been the word Mum used. Even if Chanoose was also 'subtle', she surely hadn't *chosen* to fall in love – or pretend she was in love. What possible advantage could she gain? Some form of leverage over Yaleen, through her father? Hardly! – unless Chanoose was thinking in terms of when the balloon returned; and even so, she carried more clout in her official capacity than she could bring to bear as a sort of erotic 'stepmother' . . .

There remained the possibility that Chanoose was deliberately presenting a pattern – an unstable one – which she knew would find an echo in Yaleen's behaviour . . .

No. Chanoose must have been emotionally snared at about the time that Yaleen landed on the west bank; when the world shook slightly and all hearts paused, as though in tribute to the peace mission.

Yaleen climbed into bed; and slept too deep for dreams, or for dreams to survive the dawn undrowned.

Just three weeks later, of a Tauday morning, a crowd gathered out at the big workyard at the eastern end of Capiz Street.

The majority of people present were sightseers pure and simple, for the *Pecawar Publicizer* had done as its name implied in honour of the launch. Others were more directly involved, including men of the aquaguild. One of the duties of the aquaguild was, of course, to douse any serious fires which accident might spark off in Pecawar, fires too fierce for neighbours to quench; and the aquaguild boss – having done some homework – was dubious of the wisdom of lighting a hot-air breeder anywhere near three bags full of watergas.

'If your *Rose* does conflagrate on take-off,' the aquaboss

was saying to Hasso, 'it'll drag a torch right across those houses there.'

The trio of gasbags already bobbed slackly overhead, straining slightly southward in a gentle breeze. The day was sunny, almost cloudless. The *Gavotte* rose which Tam had painted on the first stage – the hot-air globe – was the height of a tall man. *Gavotte* was a high-centred bloom of warm pink, renowned for keeping its shape for ages. Might the balloon likewise keep in shape.

'Mistress Chanoose intervened. 'Don't worry about it, Aquaboss. I doubt if these adventurers would intentionally fly a bonfire through the sky! And if that happens – which it won't – I'm sure your fellows are up to soaking any wreckage; even out here where your 'ducts drip the last drops of river-juice.'

A sly put-down, this, implying a contrast between the authentic river, plied by women, and this model river running tamely around town in brick courses. The aquaboss shrugged and turned away.

Yes, Chanoose was present. How could she fail to be, when Yaleen represented her guild? This was the first occasion since Yaleen's return to Pecawar that she had been in close proximity to her dad's mistress; and Yaleen really scrutinized the woman, limning her in her mind.

Undoubtedly Chanoose was a handsome woman. She was tall, with short curly flaxen hair, an oval face of clear skin, and sapphire eyes of the first water. Her nose was slender, though her lips were large and fleshy in sensual counterpoint. Her fingernails were long and well-mani-cured, as if to emphasize that whenever *she* worked at something physical, she never worked clumsily; nor need anyone else. Yaleen tried to imagine those nails teasing her father's buttocks, urging him; but she couldn't quite succeed.

Chanoose stared clear over other heads, to where Mum

and Dad were lurking near the back of the crowd. Mum, hiding in her belly the jewel of a new life, wouldn't stray any closer to the *Rose*, whose dangerous gasbags even now towered high as a hoganny.

'Excuse me,' Chanoose said, 'I should pay my respects to friends.' She departed, Dad-wards.

'And excuse *me*!' said a gnome of a man. 'I'm from the *Publicizer*.'

Yaleen wasn't inclined to give any more dumb interviews; and besides – 'All aboard!' shouted Tam from the gondola door – the balloon was about to depart.

The hot-air breeder was lit; which made the crew swelter somewhat and long for the cool of the sky-heights. The gasbags were swollen full of watergas, straining erect. Tethers were cast off – and the *Rose* climbed swiftly away from the eastern suburb.

Since the south-by-south-east drift was gradual by comparison, the crew had many minutes to admire the spread of the whole town.

'Oh this is the way to make maps!' crowed Hasso. 'If only there was some means of fixing quickly what we're seeing.' But there wasn't any such way. He dug Tam in the ribs. 'If only you could glaze this spectacle on to the window-glass.'

'Then we shouldn't be able to see where we're going, the rest of the time,' Tam pointed out.

Yaleen mainly had eyes for the thin red veins of the aqueduct system. These seemed to print upon the town a single complicated, curlicued letter from some unknown alphabet of signs. Or maybe it was a whole word in such a sign system. A name. A signature, which she wasn't able to decipher. The higher they ascended, the less visible this word became. It soon disappeared into the shrinking tapestry of the town, one set of threads lost in a bigger pattern which diminished quickly. Spice farms below were tiny patchworks. Away to the west, the river was but a glossy road.

'How does it feel to be a heroine?' Tam asked Yaleen.

'I think,' she said, 'I already was one.'

'Uh?'

'I feel as if I already did something splendid and awesome! But I've no idea what! I can't ever know what it is – because, because it surrounds me on all sides. It's the air I breathe. It's everything. There's nothing else apart from it.'

'That's a psychological condition known as *dayjar view*,' remarked the woman Melza from Jangali. 'When you tipple too much in the heat of the day, suddenly it seems as if things that are taking place, have already taken place before. This can occur in your dreams, too. You're convinced you're revisiting the dream – not viewing it for the first time. It happens to everyone at least once in their lives. *Dayjar view*.'

'Oh,' said Yaleen.

Presently they were high enough to enter the airstream blowing from the west. With a lurch and a bump and a twist about, the *Rose* changed course and picked up speed.

A panic breathlessness assailed Yaleen. However, she stood still and breathed slowly and pretended to herself that the *Rose* was merely afloat upon preternaturally clear water – and that a solitary cauliflower cloud down below was only a reflection of itself.

Before long they were crossing a featureless light brown plain. Beyond that plain long ridges of dunes, toothed with arrow-heads of sand, webbed the surface.

The invisible living current of air swept them onward, eastward.

Afterword

Thus it was in the time of Yaleen of Pecawar – perhaps!

Nowadays, of course, the whole of our planet has long since been thoroughly explored and thoroughly settled. We have launched machines and a handful of people into orbit around our world. There's serious talk of sending ships of space out to visit the moons of great distant gaseous Hepseba which shares this sunspace with us; though such a voyage would last for many years. Hepseba is so far away that it went unheeded by our ancestors. Some day in the distant future we might even go further, inconceivably further, to the stars to plumb the mystery of our origins.

Meanwhile we confront the mystery of these three texts discovered inside a fallen obelisk – twin to the so-called Obelisk of the Ship, buried by sand near the eastern edge of the Oriental Erg.

The Book of the River is an ancient printed volume. *The Book of the Stars* is a roll of antique newsprint tied with twine. *The Book of Being* is a bundle of manuscript papers written in three distinct and separate hands. Whereas most other ancient paper has perished over the centuries, down the millennia, these three examples were preserved by the dryness of the desert – and by their hiding place within mortared stones, which themselves were hidden inside a dune.

To say that we question the veracity of these texts is the wildest understatement. We well know that our ancestors were great romancers. (Admittedly, so are we; though nowadays we at least strive to be self-consistent in our flights of fancy!) And we know how they lived in an age of taboo and superstition – not forgetting the fungus-spore amnesiplague, which we have eradicated.

Yet why should these three documents in particular have been considered valuable enough to pack inside that obelisk? And considered so, by whom?

Had the erectors of that stone finger in this quixotic location simply found themselves one block short? Thus one of the construction crew, who happened to be a devotee of romances, used a book and a roll of newsprint and a manuscript continuation of those first two tales, as wadding to stuff into the vacant central space. And perhaps all the masons involved were romancers, since it's a romantic endeavour to rear a column of stones in a desert where it can only serve as a landmark to itself alone! Besides, as I say, at least three hands were involved in composing the third volume.

But now consider: if the first two printed books are 'true', then the third book cannot possibly be true. And vice versa. Yet if the third book alone were true, how could it have been written? Most of it would have lacked foundations (much like the obelisk!).

Only the final section of *The Book of Being* strikes us as familiar in its portrayal of our world. On the other hand, all of the persons in this last part – barring one or two minor figures – are already established in the first two books.

And what of the section written in the second hand (and second person), entitled 'All the Tapestries of Time'? Perhaps here we have a curious and cavalier attempt to connect the first two volumes with the reality of 'The Rose Balloon'. Perhaps this part was scribbled by one bored, though ingenious, stone mason whilst the construction crew sheltered in their tents during freak sandstorms. Let us imagine this author comparing notes constantly with a rival mason and would-be romancer who was busily scribbling the final part during those same storms. Both of them took as their starting point two genuine romances of the period. The first had been printed as a proper book. The second had been issued more cheaply – or more popularly? – on newsprint. And of course a partial continuation already existed in manuscript alone; which they happened to have with them in their tents. From which fact, do we deduce that a *third* mason was the original author – but he had run out of steam, and cared so little for the final product that it was left abandoned inside the obelisk as makeweight? Or that the masons feared they would die in the desert, and felt so proud of their collaboration that they sealed it inside the stones for safety?

Perhaps this is the explanation of *The Book of Being*.*

As to the content of the first two volumes, what can one say? Except, to begin with, that in many respects our ancestors viewed the world upside-down! Thus the Tambidala River flows 'down' to the north. Knowing only one river, they didn't feel the need to give it a special name; but being the only one, it was the norm. Now that we're acquainted with the other major rivers on our planet – all of which flow otherwise, from north to south – we would phrase this differently.

Secondly (and more important) through no fault of their own our ancestors were taboo-stricken; and being great romancers into the bargain they often thought mythically and metaphorically when treating taboo topics.

---

* In recent avant-garde numerology I believe there is a trick called 'renormalization', whereby so-called 'false infinities' – essential to the manipulation of esoteric theories of the universe – are subsequently got rid of, *purged*, so that an equation collapses back like a babel-house of cards into a single expression, presenting a single world, a single order. Temporarily an equation possesses an infinite solution – then suddenly a finite, graspable one emerges. I fancy that my (admittedly imaginary) masons may have been the precursors of such tricks, in words rather than in algebra. How they must have adored a concrete solution – to have set that stone finger amidst a shifting sea of sand!

Thus the 'black current' is a picturesque metaphor – a myth – used to express certain inhibitions which were programmed into us originally; which were built into our two core societies (on the east and west banks of the Tambidala) when this world was first colonized, as a way of ensuring our survival along lines presumably different from those of our mysterious mother world.

Likewise the 'Godmind' is a myth representing our designers.

Likewise the epidemic of forgetting when Godmind and 'Worm' first battled (an earthquake of the mind which is echoed later on by the final scribe's 'Pause') reflects the spore-derived amnesiplagues which caused chaos at widely separated epochs in our consequently tattered and fragmented history.

Such examples could be multiplied.

Yet curiously, as myth these texts aren't as heroic in sum as one might expect of ancient days. They also mock themselves, especially when the final 'stone-mason scribe' – in the process of purging the story of false infinities – chooses to make Yaleen marginal and submerged, rather than some hidden ruler of the world cloaked in disguise. Perhaps what we witness here (and elsewhere) is transitional myth: the withering of myth into ironic fancy in face of early industrialization and science.

Finally, '*Ka*-space' is a myth for some hyper-reality or dimension, as yet unforeseeable by us – through which the original starship must have flown.

Might not '*Ka*-space', as envisaged by the Yaleen author, seem a dangerous myth today? One which might bring superstition back into the popular mind, to oust our rational sciences? How can we contemplate *Ka*-space when our greatest dream is to launch a puny ship, our best, to the world next door – on a journey of *many years*? *Ka*-space would dwarf our efforts.

Yet the imagination needs uplifting. Joy is not to be sniffed at. So therefore let these three books be printed out of our own resources, and enjoyed.

– *'Mistress Charmy-Chateline,*
Guild of Boats & Spaceships
(advised by Savant Perse-Kirsto)